W9-AHL-723

WHERE WOLF IS KING, GOOD MEN DIE!

The big man turned his malevolent attention once more to the girl. She appeared to be feverishly attempting to load a Colt revolver. Leaning across the counter and laughing uproariously, the giant slapped it out of her grasp.

"You wouldn't try to hurt me, girlie," he taunted. His rumbling voice turned ugly. "Let's quit the horsing around, shall we?"

Lyte Majors watched this from a position well inside the door, but the big fellow must have caught a faint movement from the corner of his eye, for he jerked back suddenly . . .

"What are you up to here?" Lyte whipped out. "You lowdown horse thief! You're the man that stole my horses!"

Shaking with rage, Lyte fumbled for his gun, but the big man had his out in a flash and fired point-blank. With a gasping cry, Lyte Majors wilted loosely down in a tangled sprawl.

Other Avon Books by
Peter Field

DIG THE SPURS DEEP
GUNS FOR GRIZZLY FLAT
GUNS ROARING WEST
MAN FROM ROBBER'S ROOST
RIDE FOR TRINIDAD!
WAR IN THE PAINTED BUTTES

Coming Soon

OUTLAW DEPUTY
RAWHIDE RIDER

Avon Books are available at special quantity discounts for
bulk purchases for sales promotions, premiums, fund raising
or educational use. Special books, or book excerpts, can also
be created to fit specific needs.

For details write or telephone the office of the Director of
Special Markets, Avon Books, Dept. FP, 105 Madison Avenue,
New York, New York 10016, 212-481-5653.

A POWDER VALLEY WESTERN

COUGAR CANYON

PETER FIELD

AVON BOOKS 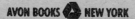 NEW YORK

AVON BOOKS
A division of
The Hearst Corporation
105 Madison Avenue
New York, New York 10016

Copyright © 1962 by Jefferson House, Inc.
Published by arrangement with Thayer Hobson & Company
Library of Congress Catalog Card Number: 88-91357
ISBN: 0-380-70710-1

All rights reserved, which includes the right to reproduce this book
or portions thereof in any form whatsoever except as provided by the
U.S. Copyright Law. For information address Thayer Hobson & Company,
P.O. Box 430, Southport, Connecticut 06490.

First Avon Books Printing: April 1989

AVON TRADEMARK REG. U.S. PAT. OFF. AND IN OTHER COUNTRIES, MARCA
REGISTRADA, HECHO EN U.S.A.

Printed in the U.S.A.

K–R   10   9   8   7   6   5   4   3   2   1

1.

THREE weary riders drew rein on a wild, rocky slope overlooking a magnificent prospect of canyons, buttes and timbered ranges in western Colorado. In the wide-flung wilderness below them, the only signs of movement were some circling hawks and the nodding of gnarled pines in the ceaseless wind.

"It just doesn't make sense to me," one of the trio said disgustedly. "Majors wrote us his ranch laid back of the San Juan peaks, and there wasn't another spread in miles. He seemed *sure* we'd locate it right off."

"He was right about one thing," growled a stocky, rotund little man clad in hide-tight bib overalls.

"What would that be . . . Mister Sloan?"

Sam Sloan's beady black eyes flashed hostilely for a moment. Then he drawled, "If we find so much as a sod shack in the next hundred square miles, it's bound to be the Slash S—I'll grant you that."

The first speaker, a one-eyed man, tall and lean to emaciation, regarded Sloan with venomous disfavor. "Said the same thing, didn't I?" he began truculently.

"No! You said it was easy," Sam snorted.

Partners for time out of mind in the little Bar ES horse ranch in Powder Valley, it was typical of the two crusty hardshells to bicker bitterly over less than nothing. Ez started to make a blistering response, only to stop.

"Let it go, Ezra." The third man of the group spoke up firmly. "The Slash S can't be far. If we keep looking we'll find it while you two are chewing about it."

1

Hazing the tarp-laden pack horse ahead of him to cover his disgruntled feelings, Ezra said no more. They pushed on down the hills keeping a careful watch.

There was a dubious frown on Sam Sloan's usually serene face. "What about it, Stevens?" he spoke up at last. "If Majors has got a bunch of horses we ought to spot the stuff grazing these slopes, hadn't we?"

Pat Stevens gave him a long look. "What have you got in your mind now?"

"Why, it looks from here as if Lyte Majors is a liar from way back!"

Shrugging his broad shoulders, Pat said calmly, "It doesn't necessarily follow. Lyte could be holding his horses in one of these canyons." Although younger than the two partners by nearly a dozen years, Pat had a level-eyed authority which the rough-barked old raw-hides usually didn't dispute.

"Hey! That's right," Ezra agreed. "Safer in this country too, from what I hear."

An hour later and some miles farther on, Ez drew up to gaze doubtfully toward a tumbledown log cabin standing forlorn and silent on the edge of a sage-cluttered bench. One corner of the weathered log walls had begun to sag, and the sod roof was disintegrating. "That can't be Majors place," he grumbled. "Nobody living there. It looks more like an abandoned line camp."

Riding up to it, they looked about. The place was puzzling. There were hoof marks, not too recent, in front of the cabin, yet the slab door stood partly open and the corrals were empty.

"Hello the house!" Ezra raised a gruff hail. "Are you here, Majors?"

The only answer was dead silence. Sitting their saddles the trio waited briefly. Ez had just started to turn toward Stevens, when a flat crack abruptly broke the peace. As if struck by an invisible hand, the lanky man's hat was torn off his head and sailed to the ground.

Whirling their broncs apart, the three raked their surroundings sharply. "Hold it!" It was Pat who saw the brush twitch a dozen yards behind the cabin. A man's slouching form took shape, his menacing rifle slanted their way as he moved into the open.

"That's a warning," came the fierce bawl. "Shear off now. On your way, do you hear?"

"Take it easy, oldtimer," Sam retorted gustily. "No call to go on the prod. We're looking for Slash S—the Majors place. You wouldn't be him, by any chance?"

"No matter." The old warrior's patience was short. "You ain't wanted here. So be off while I watch!"

"Oh, chop it off," Sam protested. "We're here to pick up those roan breeding studs you wrote us about, Majors. I'm Sam Sloan from Powder Valley." He made the introductions briskly. "This is Ezra here—and Stevens is along to help us drive the stock."

Obviously expecting this explanation to have an immediate effect, he waited. But the other man only shook his bearded head curtly. "No roans here," he rasped. "Nor none expected. Now if you're all done talking—" He jerked the rifle barrel up suggestively.

"Hang it all!" roared Ezra. "What is this? You are Lyte Majors, ain't you—and didn't you write us about them broncs? A civil word won't cost you a cent, man!"

Majors—if it was he—only canted the rifle to bear directly on Ez. His stern lips were clamped tight.

Seeing how matters stood, Pat put in a conciliating word. "Let it go, Ezra," he advised. "The man says no horses. That's plain enough. We'll just look for your breeding stock somewhere else."

His lean face dark as a thundercloud, Ez bent down from the saddle to retrieve his hat. It was not his custom to accept such treatment. Poking a blunt forefinger through the ragged tear in the hat's brim, he gave the rancher an ugly stare. "Whoever you are, don't never do that again, old terrapin—"

"I'm plumb tired of waiting," was the uncompromising rejoinder. "Next time I won't miss, if that's what you mean. Will you git?"

The trio exchanged glances. Obviously there was little

to be gained here. Clapping his hat on, Ez picked up the reins and turned his pony. "I sure don't fancy camping here anyhow! Let's shove."

Riding down off the bench in heavy silence, none of them looked back. Five minutes passed before anyone spoke. "That was the right place and no mistake about it," remarked Sam finally.

"How do you figure that?" demanded Ez.

"Spotted that Dollar brand—the Slash S—burned in the butt of a log on that cabin," Sam said.

Stevens nodded assent. "It was there. And that was Lyte Majors too. . . . Still, I don't get it," he went on soberly. "*He* knows it took us a week to get here. If he doesn't have the horses now, why not decently explain how come?"

No ready answer was forthcoming. They were still conjecturing about it fifteen minutes later when Sam held up a pudgy hand for attention. "Majors must be known on this range," he averred. "There's a hombre riding across the flats yonder. Why not ask him what the story is?" He pointed out a rider a quartermile away jogging leisurely across the dun range.

From this distance there was little to be learned about him, yet Pat's hesitation was brief. "We'll do just that," he said.

With all the mystery hovering over this range, they half expected the stranger to take flight the minute they showed themselves in the open. Instead, he swung directly toward them and came on. They presently found themselves examining a young puncher who drew up a hundred feet away and sat eyeing them warily.

"Howdy," Sam greeted him heartily.

The young fellow nodded acknowledgment without speaking.

"Maybe you can help us," Sam proceeded. "We're from Powder Valley, over east—out here to locate Lyte Majors' Slash S outfit. Back there a mile or so," he gestured behind them, "we came across a tumbledown place and an old geezer that wouldn't even talk to us. Was that Majors, or wasn't it?" He broke off to wait expectantly.

The puncher sized Sam up a little longer and then nodded grimly.

"It's him, all right," he said. "I'm Kit Majors. . . . And I suppose one of you is Sam Sloan—?"

Sam grinned. "I'm your baby. And this is my partner Ezra. Pat Stevens is along to help with those roans."

This time young Majors was even slower in replying. "Sorry, Sloan. I expect there's no question you're who you say you are. But you'll—have to overlook Pa's way."

Ezra spoke up. "That still don't get us no roan horses, boy. What about that?"

Majors shook his head. "Dad did have a herd of wild stuff we caught. He was counting on it getting us away from here and onto a real ranch—"

"What's the matter with Slash S, except that it needs some money spent on it?"

"You don't savvy." Young Majors spoke bitterly. "This is rough, lonely country—no law except what comes in from outside. Money spent on improvements here is thrown away!"

Sam immediately understood. "Owlhoots, eh?"

"They made off with our roan stock before we could get it branded," said the puncher. "We went to a world of trouble with those broncs, all for nothing."

Pat could understand how the Majorses felt. "Tough luck," he commented. "For you and us both." He scanned the barren horizon speculatively. "Where is the nearest town around here?"

The puncher jerked a thumb southward. "San Miguel. Only town inside of sixty miles, and not much at that." He seemed about to add more, only to change his mind.

"Thanks, Majors—since you can't do more for us." Sam watched the puncher turn and start away, no less circumspect of manner than before.

"That's that." Ezra grunted sourly. "So what do we do now, Stevens? Me and Sam still want horses."

Pat had never let this pair pressure him into a hasty

decision. "You can figure that one yourselves," he returned dryly. "We need supplies anyway. We'll look San Miguel over, and you might even hear of some horses for sale," he added.

This seemed reasonable and they turned in the direction indicated. Never ready to give up easily, the partners were still hopeful that something might turn up to their advantage. "Seems to be horse country all through here," Sloan offered. "We might run into a trader or two, and taking delivery on the spot, we'll be able to dicker for a good price."

"Awful anxious to spend money, ain't you?" Ez was scornful. "If this is wild horse range, why not catch our own? All it'll cost us that way is enough grub to stick around for a week or two."

Sam remained dubious. "Whooping wild horses in country we know is one thing," he grumbled. "But none of us ever saw this wild range before. . . . What do you think, boy?" He turned to Stevens.

Pat spread his capable hands. "We've done crazier things," he said thoughtfully. "I'm perfectly willing to churn around a while if that's what you want. There's one or two things I'd like to know—"

"Such as?"

Pat came out with it.

"For one thing I'd like to hear some more about those Majorses. Young Kit told a straight enough yarn. But there must be more to this than he gave out. Can a man be robbed of an entire horse herd around here without a single thing he can do about it? What *did* they do?"

The partners looked at each other soberly, arrested by this new thought. Ezra was the first to speak. "You got an argument there, neighbor. We're taking it for granted that couldn't happen to us too. Is that it?"

Sam refused to take this threat seriously. "Shucks now! We don't know how many enemies Lyte Majors has got. He's crabby enough—*I* don't class myself with him!" he chuckled. "Let's wait and see what this San Miguel has to offer."

The afternoon was waning. All three were anxious to learn more without delay, but they had only an hour or so in which to locate the village in the welter of folds and rocky ridges of which this country seemed endlessly composed.

It was sunset when they turned into a beaten trail and topped a rugged rise to look down a long brush-strewn slope upon a squat collection of adobe buildings. Without urging, the ponies increased their pace, stretching their necks forward.

In the thickening dusk the tiny village revealed itself to be one short street, poorly lit by some dim lamps glimmering through the windows of these thick-walled, low-roofed buildings. Pat looked in vain for the usual frame structure housing a supply store. There were no standing saddle horses to be seen, nor was there any saloon.

Pat's eye followed a dark-skinned figure or two clad in loose cotton clothes moving along the shadowy street. "Majors said San Miguel didn't amount to much." He grunted. "He didn't tell us it was only a Mexican village."

"Expect we can find a bait of chili beans here," Sam said unenthusiastically.

They rode the length of the street, keenly aware that they were being watched. No one accosted them.

"Huh!" Ez snorted as they turned back. "Must be an American or so living here. Only thing to do is look for one."

Dismounting near the center of town, they looked about curiously. Pat presently made out a dim figure near at hand. *"Que hombre?"* he called.

The man approached reluctantly. From his looks he was probably a herder. Stevens asked in Spanish where they could eat. There was a brief discussion, after which Pat turned toward his companions. "Let's go. We'll put on the feed bag."

They followed their guide around to the rear of a massive-walled adobe, left the ponies, and stepped inside a poorly lit room. It was smoky in here, with a fire flickering in a wholly inadequate chimney. The Mexican waved them toward a rude slab table.

A fat, dowdy woman, her inexpressive face molded of brown clay, thumped a steaming iron pot down before them. Ez had his look and scowled. "Sure enough. Frijoles," he muttered. Cold tortillas were the only available spoons, but they were old hands at this sort of thing.

Following the first generous mouthful, Sam looked up in surprise. "Say, this is sure good. *Muy bueno!*"

This artless remark broke the ice for them. The silent herder, who had been regarding them suspiciously, now showed his teeth in a grin. When they were finished and offered him a coin, he pretended to be insulted and had to be pressed to accept his pay. He even saw them to the door.

"What now?" inquired Sam, patting his prominent stomach with satisfaction.

"We need information." Ezra peered about the now dark street. "Must be a mescal joint somewhere. I'll go see." He started off.

Sam and Pat procured water for the horses from their mustached host. They waited a while for Ez to return, then set off in search of him along the dusty, gloom-cloaked street.

Sam scanned the blank adobe walls rising black against the star-shot sky. "Young Majors said this is lonely country," he grumbled. "No ranches—no law—no nothing. This town makes it seem even worse!"

"Ez must have found some place to go," returned Stevens practically. "Could be he's batting the breeze with somebody right now. We'll soon find out."

A moment later they paused in front of what was obviously a public building. A light shone from an open window inside the arcade, and the rumble of masculine voices drifted out. Moving into the shadows, they peered intently through the window.

Sam promptly snorted under his breath. "Well, good cripes! That ornery old rip didn't take long to get himself tangled up in a monte game. Him and his gambling! . . . Come on, Stevens," he growled. "We'll drag him out of that pronto!"

"No—leave him alone." Pat was unmoved by Sam's seething indignation. "Ez set out to pick up what information he could, and this may be his way. We'll give him his chance, Sam."

2.

AN HOUR later Ezra emerged from the cantina. He peered about in the darkness before discovering his friends seated on a low adobe wall near at hand. Sam slid awkwardly to the ground and the lanky man advanced.

"Nice to know you still got time for us," he rasped irritably. "Did you pick up anything?"

"Plenty." Ez was enthusiastic, ignoring his partner's crusty attack. "You weren't wrong, Stevens! This *is* wild horse range, and a good one. What's more, I know where to find 'em. So how's that?"

"That's something anyway," Sam conceded grudgingly.

Pat, on the other hand, was interested in the details. "Did you run into some American in that place?" he asked.

"No," Ezra said. "Just a bunch of Mexicans that drifted up this way from the Santa Fe country following the grass. Sheep and cattle—mostly south of here."

"Any horse hunters in the lot?" pursued Pat.

"Used to be. The Spanish *ricos* picked up a lot of prime horseflesh on this range in their day. Lately they been grazing stock and tending to their own affairs."

"Well, did you find out anything about the Majorses then?" Sam put in.

Ez grunted a negative. "They're known, of course. There's even a bunch of horse hunters from around Durango operating through here. But the Mexicans claim there's owlhoots hiding out with the horse hunters, Ste-

10

vens. Could be just superstition, but they got no use much for any of 'em on that account—and we're not specially welcome here ourselves, if you ain't caught on yet.''

Pat nodded. "It ties together. Accounts for there being no supply store, too. They don't figure to attract the flies.'' He slid off the adobe wall, resetting his Stetson. "Nothing more for us here. Shall we head for open range and bed down?''

Returning to the horses, they struck upstreet, again fully aware their progress was being followed by hidden eyes. Once San Miguel lay behind them, however, they had the lonely range world to themselves. A late moon led them to a straggling creek in a grassy fold, and they pulled up near a clump of cottonwoods. In a matter of minutes all three were wrapped in their blankets, with their ponies cropping grass nearby.

"So where's all these wild broncs at?'' Sam asked briefly the following morning, while they sipped their steaming coffee.

Ezra stood erect to gaze north and west toward broken, rolling miles of open range country, studded with barrancas and rocky buttes, sloping steadily upward toward the pale horizon. He waved that way.

"There she is. They call it the Uncompahgre Plateau. According to yarns, it's supposed to be alive with wild horses.'' He sounded deeply pleased.

Stevens had his unhurried look and nodded. "This could be even better horse country than they say—wild enough anyhow. We'll give it a whirl.''

Done eating, they loaded the pack animal and set off. Ezra knew where to look for signs. Within an hour they began to run across tracks of unshod horses. Sam promptly brightened. "There could be a chance of grabbing those roans we want after all,'' he hazarded.

Ez laughed at him lazily. "Take it easy. We'll run into plenty of broomtails and scrub stuff,'' he warned. "What we're after is good, blooded stock.''

Before noon they had seen three bands of the wild ones, clattering across the slopes at a distance, but in each case the horses were low-grade animals, runty and stunted of growth. Ez said the tracks also showed split hoofs. Sloan's spirits, stayed high, nonetheless.

"They're here, Ez," he exclaimed jubilantly. "Where there's plenty of scrubs there's bound to be prime stock too. We'll just have to keep hunting."

Horse sign increased as they penetrated deeper into the vast, wild expanse of the Uncompahgre slope. This was indeed a wild horse paradise—due to its extreme isolation, it probably had been for a couple of centuries. Further proof came, if one were needed, when a tawny cougar sprang from the crevices of a rocky dyke, bounding away with catlike resilience at the sound of their voices.

"Did you see that!" Sam sang out.

Ez re-sheathed the carbine, which he had not used after all. "Could've got him," he grumbled. "No point in scaring them broncs for miles around though."

It was the prevalence of either horses or deer which permitted cougars to thrive on any range, and they had seen little or no deer sign as yet. This country was so broken up that most of the time they could not see far in any direction, yet their keen interest in the possibilities grew with passing time.

In early afternoon they turned a bend in a sandy wash and came upon a broad bench tufted with succulent buffalo grass. The three men were barely in the open when a trumpeting blast and a rumble of pounding hoofs startled them.

A herd of thirty or forty wild horses swept out across the bench, racing like the wind. Bounding in the lead was a mighty, proud-necked stallion of a deep roan hue, perfectly proportioned. The magnificent leader whirled and stood sentinel-like on a knoll while the band of colts and mares thundered past, plunging down over the far lip of the bench. Only when the last of his band had disappeared from sight did the stallion look back, venting a piercing scream of defiance, and then turn to follow.

It happened so quickly that the trio still sat their saddles, arrested by surprise. Sam was the first to recover. "Man, what a horse!'' he cried. "And did you see some of those mares, Stevens?'' He was frankly incredulous. "Why, that bunch alone would be worth a fortune to us!''

Taken at a disadvantage as they were, and with the pack horse in tow, there was no thought of immediate pursuit. Still, the experience put a totally different face on their prospects.

Pat turned toward Ezra. "That settles it, Ez. The stuff is here," he said soberly. "In such country as this we'll have to make careful plans. For one thing we still need grub," he pointed out. "Good as it looks, this may take us a while.''

Ez nodded. "Wouldn't believe it myself till now," he confessed. "But this is better than buying the stuff if we have any luck at all.'' He thought briefly. "There was something said in town about a cross-trail grocery store somewhere in the San Rafael hills—wherever that is. Shall we try and find it?''

They had little or no choice. Halting for a scanty meal before turning back, they discussed the situation.

"Queer we ain't run into anyone else fogging those wild bunches," commented Sam, finishing the last of his beans and wiping the tin plate with a fragment of biscuit.

Stevens glanced up. "They're here. A *dozen* horse hunters could get lost in this big scope of country," he asserted. "We'll be smart to keep an eye peeled for shod tracks though.''

"What if we do run into some of 'em?'' proposed Ez.

Pat shrugged. "So we meet. Time enough for that when it happens, but you've never been shy of meeting strangers, Ez. We're after horses," he finished quietly, "and that's that.''

Done eating, they turned back. Talk was animated now that they saw at least the possibility of success. "I sure don't savvy that Majors," mused Sam in some wonderment. "If you lose a bunch of horses in this country, so what? There's plenty more to go after!''

"Don't be too cocky," Stevens warned. "Both of the

Majorses seemed to feel it was hardly worthwhile in the first place—and that could be true enough.''

"I can tell you one thing," retorted Sam. "What horses *we* get we'll keep!''

Ezra gave him a scornful look. "I'm sure glad we got you along," he muttered sarcastically. "Not a thing to worry about now. You'll take care of us!''

It was the start of a wordy quarrel which presently wore itself out through mutual boredom. Pretending to pay no attention, Stevens found a keen relish in the wrangling of this salty pair. Only when the altercation died away did he point ahead. "That long ridge yonder could be the San Rafaels—''

Late in the afternoon they struck a faint trail looping through the scrub cedar which mounted the slope. They followed it, wondering why they met no wandering rider or herder along the way. "Sure is one lonesome range," remarked Sam. "Only it ain't just empty. Begins to seem like there's something wrong around here.'' He looked to the others for confirmation.

"You, for instance?" Ez's gibe was sufficient to shut Sam up.

They rode on through advancing dusk, keeping an alert watch ahead. Topping the ridge, the trail dipped through hollows and curbed past rocky ledges. In the last light Sam drew up on a slight rise, lifting a hand.

"Some kind of place up yonder," he announced.

A few minutes later they came upon a forlorn, weathered frame structure standing on an open flat fringed about with pines. Ezra looked it over. "Must be the place I heard about.''

"An owlhoot hangout, d'you suppose?" Sam asked.

"Whatever it is, we don't have to rush in there." Pat said temperately. "Won't cost a thing to have a look around first.''

Save for the barnlike two-story building itself, there was little enough to see. There was no corral in sight, and only a sagging sawhorse visible at the rear. If it hadn't been for the pale light leaking from two of the windows, the place would have appeared entirely deserted.

"Hitch rack along that side." Ez pointed. "It's the store, all right."

Without increasing their pace, they advanced quietly and hauled up in the building's shadow. Here they stiffly dismounted.

Looping his reins over the gnawed rail, Sloan stepped aside to peer in through a faintly illuminated window. He stood still for so long that Pat's attention was caught.

"See anything, Sam?"

Sam beckoned the others forward. "Come here," he said under his breath. "Take a gander at this—"

Stevens and Ez pressed close, gazing over his bulky shoulder. The interior of the store was dusky, and for a second or two they failed to make out what had attracted Sloan. Then, at a sharp movement inside, Pat noted the tall, rawboned man leaning across the counter and gesturing imperiously.

It was Ezra who caught a glimpse of a girl's scared face in the shadows. He grunted sourly. "Female behind the counter there—and that big loud mouth is giving her a dressing-down. Mighty big and brave, ain't he?"

Through the closed window they caught the truculent rumble of the big man's tirade. They saw him threaten the girl again with upraised, hamlike hand. Sam's snort was contemptuous. "Reckon we got here just nicely in time—" Before he could turn away to start for the door at the front, Pat stopped him.

"Hold it, Sam." Pat's admonition was terse. "Let's watch this a minute."

Exasperated, Sam saw the big man start around the end of the counter as if in pursuit of the girl. "Hang it, Stevens! He'll corner her next," he protested vigorously. "I won't stand here and watch the big lug slap her around—"

He had barely finished speaking when the store door was wrenched open from the outside, and they saw a young fellow burst in. Engrossed as they were, the trio had

not heard him arrive; but clearly he had seen through the
front windows what went on inside and was rushing to the
girl's defense.

"Come out of that, you!" He sprung across the width of
the store, making for the counter's end. Fastening a grip
on the big man's shoulder, he whirled him around violently.

"Why, that's young Kit Majors," breathed Sam.

The puncher they had met yesterday had shed his stolid-
ity with a vengeance. Despite his disadvantage in weight,
he sought with savage determination to haul the husky
giant bodily from behind the counter. For a moment the
two struggled fiercely. Cans toppled off the shelf behind
them, clattering down. Then, with an ugly roar, the heavier man gave Majors a thrust with upraised knee that sent
the puncher sprawling backwards.

Kit struggled up, still resolved to eject the intruder
somehow. With a guttural laugh the other started for him,
fist cocked. Neither paid any heed to the girl's distressed
cries. Majors ducked the first ponderous swing; then a
sweeping palm caught him broadside, knocking him over a
covered barrel. The barrel went with him, crashing to the
floor.

Kit rolled away, caught himself and rose to his knees,
picking up a can of fruit from the floor. He hurled it
desperately at the big man's head and grabbed up another.
Cursing savagely, his antagonist ducked and leaped forward before Majors could throw the second can.

It was a losing contest for the light-framed puncher.
"He ain't got the beef," muttered Sam tightly. Kit slammed
to the floor again with a thud that shook the building. The
big fellow was on him before he could marshal his wits.
Majors was game. Fighting his way up, he sought to save
himself. It was no use. With a bellow of triumphant
laughter, his assailant hurled him against the door, making
it crash and shudder.

One last time Kit staggered to his feet. There was blood
on his face, his shirt was ripped, his eyes were wild and
staring. The door stood open behind him—but he never
noticed it. Nor was he able to avert the looping blow

smashing squarely into his face. Knocked violently backward, Kit tumbled across the store porch and slid limply down the plank steps.

Things had gone far enough. With one accord, the watchers at the window turned to rush around the corner and make for the entrance. Before they had taken a dozen steps, however, a treble blast of mingled fury and condemnation brought them to a halt.

All three recognized the white-bearded, bony man who slipped from the saddle and rushed forward to where young Kit lay at the foot of the store steps. It was Lyte Majors.

Clearly old Lyte was in no mood to help his son to his feet. "Got throwed out, eh? Blast your hide, boy—didn't I tell you to stay away from here?" he scolded fiercely.

The young fellow staggered erect, half tottering. "Keep . . . out of my way, Pa," he warned doggedly. "I'm going back in there right . . . now—"

The old rancher seized Kit by the ·shoulder. "Been fighting again, have you? You're all banged up!" His tone was one of rich contempt, and resolve appeared to gather in him. "Get on home, kid. I'll settle this—you hear me?" he ordered roughly. Before Kit could offer a rebuttal, Majors thrust past him and started determinedly up the steps.

With a cry, Kit whirled after him. Catching his parent by one arm, he arrested him halfway up the steps. "No, Dad—don't go in there! You wouldn't stand a chance!"

Old Lyte slapped his restraining hand away. Stepping quickly upward, he barged across the width of the porch and plunged in at the door.

Not knowing what might happen next, Pat and his friends moved forward to join young Kit at the foot of the steps. Looking past him, they had a partial view of the interior of the store.

The defiant puncher disposed of, the big man inside had turned his malevolent attention once more to the girl. She appeared to be feverishly attempting to load a Colt revolver, grabbed hastily from a display case. Leaning across the counter and laughing uproariously, the giant slapped it

out of her grasp. "You wouldn't try to hurt me, girlie,"
he taunted. His rumbling voice turned ugly. "Let's quit
the horsing around, shall we?"

Lyte Majors watched this from a position well inside the
door. The noise the big fellow was making had prevented
him from hearing the rancher enter; but he must have
caught a faint movement from the corner of his eye, for he
jerked back suddenly. Majors glared at his broad, blunt
visage and boldly stepped forward.

"What are you up to here?" Lyte whipped out. "You
lowdown horsethief! You're the man that stole my horses!"

Shaking with rage, Lyte fumbled for his gun, but the big
man whipped out his in a flash and fired pointblank. With
a gasping cry, Lyte Majors wilted loosely down in a
tangled sprawl.

3.

As HIS father fell, Kit Majors tore wildly up the steps to the door. The Powder Valley trio were close behind him. "Watch it now, how you bust in there!" called Ezra sharply.

The warning gave Kit pause, if only for a second. He had lost his gun during the rough-and-tumble in the store and was unarmed. Sam shouldered him aside, his own Colt at the ready; together, Sloan and Pat Stevens pushed warily in through the door, prepared for whatever might be awaiting them.

At first glance the place appeared to be empty, except for old Lyte lying inert in the middle of the floor. Kit rushed to his father with a cry and kneeled beside him. Heedless of the blood that ran out from under the old man's slight frame, he sought feverishly for some sign of life.

Pat and the partners ignored this, scattering to search the shadowy interior. It seemed incredible the big killer could have disappeared so quickly, and the girl as well.

"Here she is." Craning to peer over the counter, Sam caught a glimpse of her slim form lying in the aisle. "Looks like she got knocked on the head—"

He and Ezra crowded in behind the display cases to pick her up. Having made sure the hulking renegade was not hiding somewhere in the dusky corners, Stevens turned back to the puncher.

"How is he, Majors?"

Kit looked up blankly, shaking his head in stunned disbelief. "He's gone. Dad was always sure he knew so much better than me—he called me a kid. . . . And now this!"

Carrying the unconscious girl with care, Ez and Sam maneuvered out from behind the counter. There was a drop or two of blood where her chestnut hair waved back from her forehead, and her delicately modeled face was wan. While Ezra supported her, Sam dashed a sprinkling of water from the drinking pail across her cheeks.

She gave a heavy sigh, and even young Majors got up to watch solicitously. In the momentary silence of waiting all became suddenly aware of a dull thumping, somewhat muffled, coming from somewhere in the building. But the girl's gray eyes were fluttering open, so they delayed investigation.

Pat drew a rawhided chair from a corner, pushing it forward. "Sit her down," he told the partners. "She's coming out of it now. Who is she, Majors?"

"Bobby Durgen," supplied Kit dully. "She runs the store for old Ducks—"

Before he ended, the faint thumping started up again. Distant as it was, there was something sharply impatient in the sound.

Pat waved a hand toward Ezra and Sam. "Go and see what that is."

As the pair moved toward an inner door, disappearing from view, the girl gasped and tried to sit up. Stevens steadied her. "Easy does it, sister." Gently he offered her the dipper. "Just what did happen to you anyway?"

Wincing, Bobby started to lift a hand to her head. "I was—struck—" Her eyes fixed on Pat's strange face and widened in alarm. Then the sight of Kit Majors standing near at hand reassured her. "Are you—all right, Kit?"

His nod was gloomy.

"Thank goodness! I was afraid you were . . ." Suddenly she sat upright in fresh alarm. "Father! I heard him calling. Oh, I hope nothing's happened to him!" She tried to rise, only to sink back weakly.

"Hold on now," Pat soothed her. "We've got to patch up that head of yours. It looks pretty much as if you'd had a good clip with a gun barrel. If that's your dad doing the pounding," he added, "we'll know all about him directly."

At that moment a clatter sounded and Sam and Ez came staggering in. Between them they carried an armchair in which a white-headed old fellow sat. Waving a knobby cane in one bony hand, he had the fierce look of an old eagle.

"What's going on here?" His voice crackled with anger, and he nearly bounced out of his seat when he caught sight of Lyte Majors' motionless form. "Set me down!" he yelled at Sam and Ez. "I heard that shooting. Lyte's gone, is he? By gravy, I'll get to the bottom of this!" He stared accusingly into the faces of the three men from Powder Valley.

"My father, Drake Durgen," Bobby murmured.

Old Ducks however, would have none of the amenities. "Which one of you did this?" he rasped savagely.

"My name is Stevens, Durgen," Pat's voice was calm. "These are my friends." He introduced Sam and Ezra. "We got here barely in time to see the end of this. I don't know too much myself. Maybe young Majors or your girl can tell us more." He turned. "Who was that husky bird, Bobby? Did you know him?"

"It was Idaho Towner again, Father," Bobby forced out. "I've told you he's been—persecuting me for a month past. This time he was worse. Mr.—Majors came in the door and Towner shot him in cold blood. Then he came toward me. I thought he meant to kill me!"

"Idaho again, was it?" Helpless in his chair, Durgen seemed about to burst with apoplectic fury. "Dang it, girl! You had orders to lock the door on him—!"

"I'm afraid Towner was aware of our intention," Bobby said. "He stepped inside before I knew he was anywhere about."

Kit nodded. "I spotted him going in the door just as I came up," he muttered. "I didn't see his horse. He must have hidden it somewhere."

Pat was following this talk with careful attention. "Is there any chance Towner is still hiding somewhere on the place?" he interjected, glancing toward Bobby.

Old Ducks shook his head. "She wouldn't know—Towner made sure of that! . . . I did hear feet thumping out the back way a minute after that gunshot though," he added.

Pat exchanged a look with Ez and Sloan. "We'll have a look around right now," he said. Starting for the inner doorway, he turned back at the threshold. "Look after the Durgens for a few minutes, will you, Majors?"

At the moment Kit was retrieving his six-gun from where it had fallen under the counter. He straightened up with an angry nod, looking much as if he would have liked to use the weapon. "I'll do that," he said curtly.

"Better make it quick, Stevens." Sam followed Pat impatiently into the back hall. "We're wasting time while this Towner character's covering ground on the jump."

Pat was not to be rushed, however. "Let's not get ahead of ourselves. Grab that lantern there in the corner," he said coolly. "We'll make sure Idaho's not hiding somewhere here in the building. . . . I know—" he headed off Sam's vigorous protest. "We could be too late if we fool around. But it would be stupid to rush out of here and let that hombre cut in behind us. From what I've seen already, I wouldn't put it past him!"

Touching a match to the lanterns, they went through the frame building methodically, searching every nook and corner upstairs and down without bringing the renegade to light.

"Okay. Douse the lanterns, and we'll comb the yard." Stevens stepped through the back door, followed by the others. For a brief space they listened alertly. No clatter of horse hoofs, however faint, came to their ears. Sam made it a point to see that their own horses were safe. He came back shaking his head. "Towner didn't go that way."

At the far edge of the flat a fringe of pine and spruce loomed dimly against the stars. "That must be where he left his bronc," Pat said. They started that way, probing the shadows. An owl's lonely hoot startled them once, but no other sound disturbed the heavy night quiet.

Walking into the clump of trees, Pat sniffed the air. Almost at once he detected the acrid odor of horse droppings. "Touch off that lantern again, Ez."

The lanky man raked a match on his pants, and the lantern flared. By its light they scanned the ground and quickly located the spot where a lone horse had stood. Ezra followed the marks of its departure for a few yards. Then he turned back. "That was him," he announced briefly. "Took off on the tear, too. He's probably several miles away by this time."

Pat had learned to rely implicitly on the one-eyed tracker's readings of trail signs. "Nothing more we can do about him tonight in that case," he ruled. "Worth it to know Towner's not still hanging around though." He was silent as they went back toward the store. "I want to talk to Durgen some more," he said at last. "Maybe we can find out something about this bird Towner."

Kit and the Durgens were waiting with poorly concealed uneasiness when they reentered the store. "Well! Find anything?" barked old Ducks challengingly.

Pat spread his capable hands. "We saw where his horse was hidden out in the scrub. He's gone."

Pat noted that the three exchanged looks of undisguised relief. His feeling that these natives knew much that they preferred not to divulge grew stronger. Kit Majors gave him no time to speak.

"I hope you intend to take Towner's trail, Stevens!"

"Me?" Pat chose not to understand his meaning. "Not at all. I never had any dealings with the man, Majors, and I can't say that I want to."

"But blast it all! You saw him murder my father. You're a witness—!"

The words appeared to start a fresh train of thought in Pat's mind. "That's right." Now he came out with a direct question. "Exactly what reason *did* Towner have for killing your father? Lyte said: 'You're the man who stole

my horses!' Were those the broncs he gathered for us,
boy?'' he asked keenly.

"I don't know what he intended to do with them." Kit's
brevity revealed his wariness.

"You told us the roan horses Majors gathered were
stolen," Pat persisted. "*He* told us there wasn't a bronc
left on the place! If they weren't our horses, what goes on
here?"

"They were your horses," Kit allowed after a delay.
"And Idaho Towner's got them!"

Understanding Kit's resentment, Ezra turned to the scowling storekeeper. "Who is this Towner anyhow, Durgen?"
he demanded.

"He's a danged renegade, and a thief and a killer, o'
course," old Ducks ripped out shrilly. "Do you need to
ask?"

Ez glared at him angrily. "Mighty careful of what you
all say, ain't you?" he rasped. "So far we ain't been told
a thing we don't already know—but we're expected to
rush out and hunt this wolf down." Silence followed this
blunt speech. "Still some question of who's being made a
fool of here, if you ask me."

Despite his helplessness, Durgen had a fighting spirit.
"You're taking the words out of my mouth," he snapped.
"Who are you for the matter of that? You saw this killing
in my store and never raised a hand to stop it. It ain't your
fault my daughter ain't right where Majors is either! But
when it comes to calling Idaho Towner to account, you're
not interested." He was breathing stertorously, but he
didn't let up. "For all *I* know you're part of Towner's
crowd, mister—and being mighty careful to cover up for
him!"

If indignation were fatal, Ezra's look could have killed
him. Pat broke the angry silence, speaking moderately.
"You've got an argument, Durgen. But Majors here will
tell you who we happen to be. We came over here to pick
up a horse herd that Lyte Majors offered for sale," he
explained, "and we're well enough known in Powder
Valley. We were a shade too late, it seems—and Majors

himself wouldn't even explain to us. Maybe he had reason to drive us off the Slash S with a gun. Still, even you can see that doesn't make us too anxious to go after his killer.''

Old Ducks was only partially mollified. "If I had two good legs, I wouldn't take no time to split hairs about it.''

"Then look at it this way.'' Stevens still did not raise his voice. "Would you rush off and leave that girl here in the store—which is what you and Majors are asking us to do?''

"Pah! Towner's long gone from here if that's what you're worrying about,'' Durgen scoffed.

"You hope so,'' corrected Pat coolly. "Just remember that, as near as we know, Towner thinks your daughter is the only witness to the murder of Lyte Majors. He didn't take time to finish her off, but once he gets thinking about it, what do you think he'll do?''

Durgen's frozen look betrayed his startled reaction. Even Kit's eyes widened in horror. "Stevens, you're smarter than I am,'' he exclaimed self-accusingly. "Still—couldn't you leave me here on guard?''

Pat thought it as well not to remind the puncher of his proven ineffectiveness where Idaho Towner was concerned. Ignoring the query, he turned back to old Ducks.

"As for our being spies for Towner,'' he declared, "I never laid eyes on the man before tonight, and I certainly didn't know what to expect of him. For that matter, *he* never saw us at all—which could be worth something to us sooner or later.'' He paused. "From your talk, Durgen, Towner might be the head of an outlaw gang that operates around here. Last night in San Miguel Ezra picked up the rumor that big time owlhoots are believed to be hiding out with the Uncompahgre horse hunters. Isn't it only too likely that Towner could be one of them?''

Durgen waved his cane irately. "He never showed me his credentials. But he couldn't be nothing else!'' he averred. "All *we* know is, he's been hanging around pestering Bobby! She says he's been getting bolder. He left his trademark this time, and no mistake!'' His fierce eyes strayed to Majors, still lying where he had fallen. "Once this gets out, we'll lose what little trade we got."

"Couldn't the law be called in to straighten things out?" demanded Sam. "Sure seems like it's time for it."

"A deputy might drift in here next fall from Durango—if he wasn't busy," Durgen said bitterly. "Would that help?"

"If there was a definite charge to press that would make a difference." Pat was practical. He turned suddenly. "If you're ready to talk, Majors—?"

Kit struggled briefly with his anger. "I told you Idaho Towner stole Dad's horses," he burst out hotly. "It happened I was away that day. Dad told me he swapped lead with a couple of hombres and was driven out of Chisos Canyon. He wouldn't say any more, but an unguarded remark gave him away. It was Towner all right—and Dad was planning to square accounts!"

"No case there," Ez growled.

Majors understood as much. "Do we need any stronger case than we've got? Do we *have* to wait? There's just one way to settle this, Stevens. And that's to run this rabid dog down and stomp him into the ground!"

"Well." Pat was markedly temperate. "I can understand how you feel. But there's the little matter of what Towner will think up before you overhaul him, boy, not to mention dealing with him once he's caught. If I've got it straight, not many men can tap him on the shoulder and say, 'Come along.' . . . Meanwhile there's your father to be taken care of," he reminded Kit. "You're not forgetting him, are you?"

Kit flushed. "Let's say it's because I didn't that I was fool enough to expect something of you," he retorted caustically. "You're a strange person, Stevens. You think mighty straight one minute, and then turn sarcastic the next!"

Pat's nod was unperturbed. "It's a fact that I'm my own boss, and I don't stampede easy. Is that what you mean?" Without awaiting Kit's reply, he turned to Ezra and Sam. "Help him pack Majors out and put him on his horse, boys," he suggested quietly.

Kit looked as if he would have preferred to refuse their aid, but he had no choice. Together, they toted Lyte's limp form out and down the steps. It took time to fasten the body across the saddle. Pat came out to join them. He watched Kit crawl stiffly astride his own pony and take the reins of the other horse.

"Try to use common sense about this, Majors," he said before the puncher could turn away. "You're bound to feel revengeful toward Towner, of course. But don't make any foolish attempt to track him down. That could be just what he's waiting for, and you'll only be asking for worse trouble."

"Easy for you to talk," flashed Kit. "You've only to ride away, pick up your damned horses somewhere else, and you're well out of the whole business!"

"So what do you intend to do?" Pat challenged him sharply.

"Never mind! I'll do what I have to. But you'll never hear how it came out, so why worry?" With this parting shot, Kit Majors turned his pony out and started home, leading his father's horse with its melancholy burden.

4.

PAT thoughtfully watched young Majors fade into the gloom and then turned back to Ezra and Sam. "He's on the prod now. He'll think over some of the things said to him," he predicted, "and cool off."

"I don't know," Ez said dubiously. "If Towner figures him for a witness as well as that girl, his life won't be too easy."

"That's right," seconded Sam. "Towner may hide out a while, but it's my guess he'll be back. That hombre is bad news all around."

Moving toward the store as they talked, they dropped the subject as they neared the steps and started to enter. Bobby Durgen was already scrubbing the floor while old Ducks sat glowering in gloomy thought. "Here. Give me that mop." Sam brusquely relieved the girl of her unsavory task.

Durgen took note of the action, nodding. "Go and stir up some supper, girl," he ordered. "I reckon you'll stay over—?" he said to Pat.

"We stopped by to pick up some supplies," Pat said "There's nothing to drag us away overnight."

The men talked while Bobby was busy in the kitchen. Far from garrulous as a rule, the helpless store proprietor kept up a terse commentary. It finally struck Stevens that Durgen was working around to some subject. Finally, he came out with it: "You rode over here to pick up some horses from Majors—that's out now. So what'll you do about it, Stevens?"

"I gather this is real wild horse range," responded Pat. "Nothing to prevent us from taking a whirl at making our own gather. We figured we'd have a look around."

Durgen pouted his lips sternly. "There's horse hunters working over there in the Uncompahgre," he objected.

"Yes. But there's lots of room over there, oldtimer. That needn't interfere with us."

"I wouldn't be too sure of that—"

"They're likely to give us trouble, you mean?" Pat didn't take the suggestion seriously. "We're used to looking after ourselves."

Old Ducks, who had measured them shrewdly ever since he had first laid eyes on them, looked as if he could believe it. Nevertheless, he shook his head irritably. "Well, it ain't only what you *know* you're up against," he argued. "If you're wise, you'll keep an eye open for the things you don't even expect!"

Ez shot the old fellow a keen look. "That the way things are here?"

Durgen expressed his prime disgust by a twitch of his cane. "I was lucky to find this business after I got thrown from a wagon three or four years ago," he growled. "My girl talked me into it, and she does most of the work. Even at that things were going all right till this—this danged—"

"Till Towner showed up. Is that it?" Sam put in.

"He's played hob with my living, Sloan! Business never was too good here. Since he started to haunt us, it's been going down and down."

"Bobby said something about him hounding her," Pat interrupted the old man's tirade. "You can't mean Towner is around here that much?"

"Not only that," Durgen fired back. "He seems to be playing a game with us, Stevens! What he done to Kit Majors is nothing unusual. Towner's picked quarrels with one customer after another. He's a big overgrown ox— nobody's flattened him yet. Lately he's even started bringing his tough cronies here with him. They carouse around at their own sweet will, and the devil with me. I've seen customers turn around and go back, seeing that gang around here!''

Pat was trying to puzzle it out in his unhurried way. ''Idaho must have some object in all this,'' he pointed out. ''He'd hardly go to all that trouble unless he stood to gain by it.''

''Could be a scheme to make this an owlhoot hangout,'' Ezra said soberly. ''If he fixes it so respectable range folks stay away, he's safe.''

''Did he or anyone else ever make you an offer for the store, Durgen?'' Pat inquired.

''The way things are, he likely figures he'll drive me out,'' old Ducks answered bitterly.

Sam shook his head. ''Not the best place in the world for a young girl at that,'' he allowed.

Before more could be said, Bobby called cheerfully from the kitchen that supper was ready. Ezra and Pat carried Durgen's chair to the table. The trio found a water basin and towel outside the back door and cleaned up a bit.

By common consent the subject of Idaho Towner was dropped for the girl's sake. She seemed to have taken a liking to Sam, bristly and unkempt as he was, hovering around his place; in fact, it was plain that the presence of Sam and his friends had greatly relieved her most pressing anxieties.

''Eat some more, Dad—and all of you,'' she urged. ''I expect to see thirds disappear at least!''

Sloan slapped his drumlike stomach leaning back from the table in pretended horror. ''Are you trying to make me fat?'' he demanded.

Bobby's laugh rang out. ''I could never do that,'' she declared audaciously.

Sam bounced up when the faint tinkle of the store bell threw a chill over the table. ''I'll go see who that is,'' he said.

There was a notable decline of talk while they waited for his return. He was back presently. ''Some Mex herder stopped by for frijoles and carbine shells,'' he announced in an offhanded manner. "I dumped the money in the cash drawer."

Coffee loosened their tongues again, and they discussed young Kit Majors' unfortunate situation. It was Durgen's hardboiled opinion that the puncher was better off, if he only took advantage of it. "Old Lyte was a bullheaded diehard," he averred. "He was bound to hang on there at the Slash S with nothing to hold either of 'em. If Kit drifts off to a better range and grabs a job, he may get somewhere."

"Father!" Bobby sounded shocked. "Lyte Majors was Kit's only parent. Are you implying that I'll be better off when—when you are gone?"

"That's about it." Old Ducks was grimly callous about it. "But I suppose I'll hang on a long time with these useless pins of mine!"

The girl looked helplessly at Sam and then at Pat. "If Kit is anything like I know him, he won't leave as long as his father's killer goes free," she said stoutly.

Stevens liked her spirit. Nor did it escape him that her interest in the young fellow who had rushed to her defense was a lively one. "Majors won't leave without telling you, that's certain," he assured her.

"What difference does it make?" Ducks grunted. "Them Majorses are just more grief to us. This is bound to get around and give our place a bad reputation."

"Keeping it covered up would only help Towner to get away with it," Pat pointed out quietly. "You're bound to admit the Majorses weren't asking for anything like this, Durgen."

The old man would have argued further, but the girl's downcast expression showed that privately she felt at least partly responsible for what had happened. Pat smoothly changed the subject, and not long afterward, the three made their plans for the night.

Sam and Pat took advantage of a bedroom behind the store, while Ez chose to sleep out with the horses. The dark hours passed without incident. Next morning Ezra and Sam ransacked the store, buying prodigally—it took another hour to load the pack horse. Stevens emerged from a leisurely talk with Durgen as this task was being completed.

"Sam, I'll ask you to stay with the Durgens for a day or so," he said. "Ez and I should be back by that time, and we'll know pretty much what we plan to do."

Sam's moonface went into eclipse. "Has it got to be me?" he began argumentatively.

"Why, no," the younger man responded with cool readiness. "I'll stay myself, and you and Ez go ahead. It's you two that want those horses."

The words put a different face on the situation at once. "No—go ahead." Now Sloan saw the importance Pat attached to leaving a guard at the store. If any excitement occurred here, he wanted to be in on it. "I'll make out for a day or two, if it does bore me," he said.

Stevens winked at Ezra and proceeded to saddle up. They were soon ready to leave.

"I don't suppose you'll see Kit again—?" Bobby called anxiously from the store porch.

"We'll tell him everything's quiet," Pat assured her.

Striking out at once, the pair dropped down off the San Rafaels and headed for the Uncompahgre rise, the laden pack horse trotting in their wake. It was a cool, fresh summer morning. As they rode, Ezra pointed out a catch basin or two in the rocks, where water still lay from the last spring storm. They saw tracks where a small band of mustangs had watered, and Ez shook his head.

"Water's no problem to the wild ones now," he declared. "We can't use one of these springs as a trap."

"No, but at the same time, they're less wary than they will be later," returned Pat. "When you can't find so much as a set of tracks, you know it's tough to run wild horses. There seems to be a God's plenty of them through here. Funny in a way there aren't more hunters," he went on thoughtfully, "given the amount of stock there must be from what we've seen."

"Just plain hard to drive it out of this wild country, I expect." Ez was disinclined to talk, his single eye busy.

More than once as the morning wore on, they spotted small bunches of mustangs at a distance. Near midday they ran across a band that looked better than average. There was a sturdy buckskin in the lead that took Pat's eye.

"Let's scout that bunch and find out just how skittish they are," he proposed.

They set off, circling carefully to windward of the incredibly keen-scented horses. Even when the wild ones detected no concrete threat, they remained wary. The pair were forced to ride miles to get close enough for a decent look. They soon found themselves greatly hampered by the straggling pack pony.

"Cripes! We'll have to do something different." Ez drew rein to regard the troublesome animal. "We got to stake that dog some place we'll know where to find it."

Pat showed a mildly exasperated grin. "It's either that or give up."

They found a small depression carpeted with buffalo grass and hemmed in by rocks. A stone monolith of unusual shape adequately marked its location. Here they slipped the packs and staked out the extra bronc, taking the precaution of stowing the supplies in a crevice.

"Come on boy," Ez was urgent, swinging into the saddle. "That bunch will be in Utah before we catch up."

Thrusting on with greater freedom, they once more attempted to close in on the band that had attracted them. The rugged ground and the obvious familiarity of the buckskin leader with this range gave them further trouble. Ezra at last hauled up, his lean face unusually grim.

"This is a standoff," he growled. "We won't have a chance till we start out-thinking them broomtails." He pointed a bony finger. "That ridge yonder seems to be throwing them north. We'll climb up there far enough for a look around."

Pat did not demur. When the one-eyed tracker grew dictatorial—as he often did when exasperated—it was usually for good cause. Ez was without a peer in dealing with any form of wild life, and his word was law. Turning aside, they worked up the ridge, clinging to rugged folds to avoid calling attention to their movements.

Twenty minutes later the scarred and wrinkled plain lay outspread below. They spotted the wily buckskin leading its band steadily on. Pat watched in chuckling amazement. "You could teach that horse to play checkers without much trouble," he exclaimed. "Look at how he follows the level and at the same time avoids the rock patches." It was no novelty to either of them that wild horses often showed uncanny intelligence.

Ezra scanned the rugged terrain beyond. "Looks like sort of a blind canyon in that elbow yonder—past the base of the cliffs there. If we can chivvy that bunch into the gap, Stevens, the buckskin's ours."

Pat saw the plan. "We'll have to split up and swing wide enough not to crowd them on past," he suggested. "I'll ride on around, Ez. You follow the ridge up and make sure they don't turn back."

Ez nodded. But in the midst of his planning, Pat noted that he took time to sweep his keen glance in a complete circle, studying their surroundings for any signs of movement. He saw none and waved a big hand for Stevens to proceed.

Turning back, Pat threaded his way downward. He spurred his mount to a good pace once the going improved, working east for a mile and then turning north. It was some time before he thought it prudent to climb a rocky dyke and search for the wild band. He did not see them, but well past the cliffs marking the gap in the ridge, he turned once more and began working that way.

Ten minutes later his eyes picked up the buckskin, a beautiful figure, diminutive in the distance, standing guard while its tiny band grazed an open slope comparatively free of sage. The plan appeared to be working well. Pat had only to show himself, and the buckskin would be off in a flash, its straw-colored tail whipping the breeze. The stallion was now herding its charges straight toward the V-shaped gap in the ridge. Its trumpeted warning of rage and defiance would inform Ezra that the trap was closing.

It was a matter now of making every second count. Racing forward, Stevens made sure the mustangs did not break back toward the open at the last moment.

The band of horses made the turn past the lofty cliffs with a rumble of unshod hoofs and clattered over a fold to disappear momentarily from sight. Almost at once Pat got a glimpse of Ezra waving triumphantly as he closed in from below. They had yet to discover the exact character of this stonewalled trap, which would in turn determine how they must proceed with the catch. But for this moment, the wild horses were effectively trapped.

Ez worked as close to the band as he dared, risking a yell. "Unlimber your rope!" he bellowed. "We can't hold 'em here! This'll be fast and furious once they make a break—the most we can do is grab a couple of prizes!"

Already freeing his rope from the cantle, Pat waved him back. "Make your own play," he sang out. "I'll do the same. It won't take five minutes for that bunch to find out they've been tricked!"

Pat was barely able to race up to a strategic position when he heard the thunder of racing, pounding hoofs. It seemed strangely loud—he had heard this swelling, ominous drumming during cattle stampedes—but he was utterly unprepared for the sight that burst on him a moment later.

Not a dozen, not the score or less of the wild broncs they had been chasing, but over a hundred wildly charging mustangs came pouring forward, savage heads thrown up and manes flaunting!

Startled as he was, Pat took swift note of the magnificent animals in this first fierce onrush. He knew what it spelled. All unawares, they had stumbled on some favorite hideout of the wild ones. Totally unprepared for such a stampede, they were completely unable to cope with the problem it presented.

Selecting a fiery roan stallion well worth a fight, Stevens readied his rope as the brute raced forward. But at the last second, his own pony, daunted by the cascading mustangs whose nearness filled it with terror, exploded in a

wild display of bucking and sunfishing. Pat strove to
master the animal and at the same time avoid the savage
horseflesh pouring past in a tidal wave. In a matter of
crazy seconds the equine tornado had swept past and thundered on to freedom. Choking and sneezing through the
brown pall hovering in its wake, Pat brought his mount to
an uneasy stand. It did not escape him that, like his own,
Ezra's chances of surviving such a stampede of slashing
hoofs must have been slight indeed. He was still calming
the spooked pony when a gruff hail reached him.

"Are you still there, boy? . . . Did you see something
go past?" Ez was chagrined and at the same time grimly
amused, his single eye glinting through the paste of dirt
which masked his gaunt face. "Hang it all—I never laid a
rope on one of 'em! I'm hunting horses but not a horsehide
blizzard!"

Pat's laugh was equally rueful, yet far from discour-
aged. "That was our own fault, Ez. It's mighty plain now
we don't know this range. There's a fortune in horses
here, and no mistake. But we'll have to get better orga-
nized and not go at it in any half-baked way. . . . Shall we
shove on back to camp?"

5.

"WE LEFT it right here." Ez stared about the grassy hollow in perplexity. "There's the big rock yonder—and that's the crack we stuffed the packs into. Hang it all! Could be the picket pin pulled, and the critter wandered off . . ."

It was sunset. The pair had returned to where the pack pony had been staked out, only to find it missing.

"It's mighty queer." Ez roamed about the hollow looking for tracks. The spot was sufficiently marked up, however, to be confusing. While the tall man worked out toward the edges of the little cup, Pat made straight for the place where the supplies had been cached. He had his methodical look and straightened, turning.

"You can stop hunting!" Pat's hard tone jarred Ezra. "The packs are gone too."

"Gone—?" Ez whirled in consternation. For a second, his look was blank. "They *can't* be gone, boy. You don't mean—?"

"Stolen. Along with the horse," Pat said flatly. "A staked-out bronc may stray, given the chance—it doesn't wait to pick up its packs. So there you are."

Angrily, Ez searched for the thief's tracks. He found a few which told no more than they knew already. Waning daylight soon put an end to this activity, and Ez turned back.

"Who would it be?" Pat shrugged. "Idaho Towner himself, for all I know. The point is, we're stuck without grub."

Ez had shot a rabbit on the way back. Building a tiny fire, he broiled the meat, and they dulled the edge of hunger before bedding down for the night. They talked about getting a rich haul in horses here if they played their cards right; but there was already a warning in what had happened to them. Ez was deeply resentful of the range thief. "A man don't have to steal to get along in this country if he'll work at all," he declared.

"Lyte Majors worked hard, and they stole him blind," reminded Pat. "*He* was about ready to give up."

"Well—I wouldn't put this past young Kit till I made sure," growled Ez. "We'll get back to Durgen's in the morning and scout around. We got no choice anyhow."

They were up and away early with nothing to delay them. By midmorning they were once more climbing the San Rafaels.

Two men were standing on the store porch watching keenly as they drew near. Pat recognized Sam readily enough, and a moment later spotted young Majors sitting glumly on the porch, his back against the wall. The third man, a tall individual, bigger than most, seemed vaguely familiar.

"Back early, ain't you?" called Sam as they rode near. "I don't see those wild broncs either."

Ezra's snort was one of pure disgust. "We not only got none, but lost one of our own!" His single eye fixed on the man beside Sloan. "Hey! Ain't that Ed Roman?" he lowered his voice to ask quickly.

Pat nodded. "Howdy, Roman," he called, lifting a hand in greeting.

The gimlet-eyed U.S. marshal responded bluntly. "Heard you were around, Stevens," he said. "I was waiting for you."

"How's that?" Dismounting, Pat pretended not to understand.

"Want your story of what happened here." Roman was terse. "There seems to be some confusion about it—"

"Why, Majors there could tell you everything we can," Pat said coolly.

The lawman cast a dour glance at Kit "Maybe he can, but he sure got off on the wrong foot doing it. . . . I stopped over at Slash S last night, Stevens, and this bird started throwing lead at me! I put a stop to that fast, but I don't like it."

"I told you I thought you were Idaho Towner!" Kit burst out. "It was getting dark—I couldn't see too well. And I was expecting that hombre!"

Ezra glanced briefly at Pat. If Kit had been home on the Slash S at dusk, he could not possibly have stolen their horse and packs. It settled that question decisively; but at the same time, the puncher was plainly in trouble.

"Explain to Roman what's been going on, Stevens," Kit demanded. "It was you that suggested calling in the law. Now he's here, he won't even look at Dad's grave—but he's holding *me* in custody!"

Smiling faintly, Pat gave the lawman a brief rundown of events since their arrival on this isolated range. "There's no question about Majors' murder, Roman, because we witnessed it ourselves. If Kit's been a little jumpy, that's understandable. Towner seems to be riding rough-shod over this range, and it's to be expected he might show up over there at the Slash S. If the boy didn't make an effort to protect himself, he could be wiped out the same way."

Roman heard Pat out, nodding shortly. It tallied with what Ducks Durgen had told him this morning. But he was still convinced Majors had to be held. "I can't overlook careless gunplay," he asserted stubbornly. "But I will place him in your custody, Stevens—"

"Oh no." Pat's headshake was prompt and final. "I won't have time. We're here after horses, and we expect to be busy. Majors can come with us, of course, strictly on his own." He broke off. "What brings you here, Roman?"

"Officially, I'm tracking down an outlaw crowd that stuck up a train over at Rocky Ford last month. They killed the messenger and a member of the crew." Ed was matter-of-fact about what appeared a routine assignment. "I got word some of 'em were hiding with the horse hunters around the San Juan peaks. Have you run into any of that bunch?''

Pat said no. "Except whoever it was that stole our pack pony yesterday. That could have been Towner's work too.''

Roman nodded. "He's the man I want. He's being hunted for a dozen crimes, some of them up in Wyoming.'' His eyes narrowed thoughtfully. "I suppose you're hot after this horse you lost—if nothing else?''

"Let us catch up with this Towner once and we'll show you,'' Ez interrupted hotly.

Roman turned to Pat. "How about this, Stevens? Go after Towner as my deputy,'' he proposed. "That'll release me to hunt down the rest of that gang.''

"There's your chance, Stevens,'' Kit urged vigorously. "Maybe you can even get your bronc back!''

Pat's refusal was prompt. "I won't waste time by getting involved,'' he said. "Towner's got another murder right here to settle for. He's your first job, and a big enough one too. Better get after him, Roman.''

"But dang it, Stevens!'' protested Kit. "Towner's almost certainly got a spy or two—and we know he's got friends. One man can't tackle him alone. You were careful to remind me of that!'' He had a hopeless, pleading look. "Only think! With a deputy's badge, you can blast that rat down, and no questions asked. It's no more than he did to my Dad!''

Pat seemed unmoved. "Got my work all lined up for me, haven't you? I just don't happen to be crazy for revenge right now—and I'm not working for you. As you said, the law is here. If Roman thinks you're more important than Idaho Towner, I won't argue with him.''

The federal marshal took this in without comment while his thin lips tightened under his mustache. No strangers to each other, he and Stevens had had their differences before, and Roman recalled that he had not always come out on top. "What'll you do now?'' he inquired gruffly.

"I set out to pick up a few horses with the boys,'' Pat answered. "We still figure to do that.''

Roman grunted. "It's possible you'll run into other horse hunters. So keep your eyes open, Stevens, if you don't do anything else. I'll count on you to pass on whatever you learn. Will you do that?"

"Naturally, I'll be glad to see Towner crossed off," Pat agreed. "His kind never spells anything but grief. Our first chore is to pick up a pack animal," he continued. "Durgen may know where we can find one."

"Why didn't you pick up a broomtail in the hills?" interjected Sam. "That would be good enough for what we want."

Ez gave him a pitying look. "Did you ever try to break a scrub bronc for packing?" he inquired scathingly. "We want a critter to carry our grub—not distribute it."

Sam grinned. Whatever he was about to retort was interrupted by Bobby Durgen's appearance. The girl halted in the doorway, her worried expression brightening as she saw Pat.

"I was hoping you might come back. Mr. Stevens, Father would like to talk to you if you can spare a minute."

Thinking he detected faint anxiety in her manner, Pat turned that way. "No time like the present," he remarked, mounting the steps.

Pat heard Ezra address a casual question to Roman as he and the girl stepped in the store. Once inside beyond earshot of the others, Bobby turned to him impulsively. "Pat, it was me who wanted a word with you—not Dad," she murmured quickly.

"Fine." He gave her an encouraging smile. "At your service, Bobby. What'll it be?"

"It's—about Kit Majors," she said uneasily. "He's in difficulties with Marshal Roman."

"I know." Pat nodded. "Ed was telling me about it."

She appeared anxious for Pat to comprehend fully the puncher's dilemma. "I don't blame the marshal. Kit *is* impulsive. But Mr. Roman refuses to recognize his great provocation. . . . Perhaps if you could speak to him, Pat—?" She broke off, embarrassed.

Whatever he chose to draw from the words, Pat could

scarcely mistake her grave concern for Majors. "I've given Roman a dig or two already about that," he returned. "I doubt if he aims to do anything more than throw a jolt into the boy. He says Kit shot at him—and that *was* careless."

"But don't you see? . . . Marshal Roman might be mistaking him for one of those outlaws. And that isn't the case at all!"

Pat shook his head reassuringly. "Ed's too sharp for that kind of a mistake. He wouldn't expect Kit to be running with the man who killed his father."

"He doesn't speak as if he saw that at all." Clearly, the girl felt that Pat also was being obtuse.

He patted her shoulder lightly. "Take it easy, Bobby," he advised. "Kit hasn't done anything worse than kick up his heels a bit. I know you feel sorry for him but this will iron out all right. Now if I can see your pop," he said briskly, "I've got something to say to him myself." Giving her another smile, he waited expectantly.

Still uncertain, yet inclined toward full confidence, the girl studied Pat's face for a moment; then she turned to lead the way. Ducks Durgen was sitting beside the window in a back room, a blanket over his useless legs, one veined hand resting on the top of his ever-present cane.

"Well, Stevens," he greeted Pat gruffly. "Don't tell me you got your horses already. Giving up?" he demanded shrewdly.

Pat chuckled. "Somebody wants us to." He told about the stolen pack horse and the supplies.

Durgen scowled. "Stevens, I can remember when this was empty country. It's going to the dogs now." He shook his head. "What'll you do?"

"I'll go back, of course." Pat cheerfully related his and Ezra's surprising encounter with the band of mustangs. "After that, nothing could keep those old rawhides of mine out of the Uncompahgre. I'll admit I'm interested myself. I was hoping you could say where we can pick up another pack animal."

Old Ducks looked at him suspiciously. "Ain't been

nosing around here, have you?" he growled. "Maybe you talked to my girl—"

Bobby had left them a moment ago to return to the store. "Why no." Stevens looked surprised. "Was there something she could have told me?—We didn't need a pack pony till this morning," he pointed out.

Durgen grunted. "Reckon I can supply you one if you're not fussy. . . . There's a barn in the hollow yonder," he explained. "We had to take in an old hack on a bad bill last week. I'll settle for ten dollars, Stevens—and just be sure you don't take one of my own team!"

"Fine." Pat produced the sum named, and Ducks grandly waved it away.

"Pay my girl after you've looked at that plug," he said. "You'll need more supplies anyhow. At this rate, Stevens, I'll be growing rich at your expense. If you'd rather wait till after you snag a bunch of mustangs—"

Pat smiled. "After riding over here in the expectation of paying Lyte Majors for a herd of matched roans, a few supplies won't even make a dent in our pocketbook."

"Well, keep a close watch on it." Ducks waved him away as if no longer interested, and returned to his own preoccupations.

Walking back into the store, Pat's thoughts were busy. After pausing at the counter long enough to acquaint Bobby with the arrangements about the pack horse, he moved to the door. "Sam," he called. "Will you help Bobby pick out the fresh supplies we'll need?"

The stocky man stepped over to the doorway. Ez was still talking to Kit Majors and Roman at the edge of the porch. Lowering his voice, Pat spoke so that only Sam could hear him. "I've got a bronc. As soon as it's packed, I want you and Ez to put the clamps on young Kit—we'll haul him along with us whether he likes it or not. I'll keep Roman out of the way, and you can wait down the trail for me."

Sam solemnly winked and passed on into the store. Pat stepped out as Ezra and the two other men turned toward him.

"Ez, we're buying a pack horse from Durgen," he annunced. "It's out in the barn—Kit will show you. Will you go after it?"

"Well, that's good." Eager for immediate action Ezra started down off the steps.

Young Majors hurried to catch up. "This way, Ezra—" He was glad to get out of Roman's sight even momentarily.

Pat watched them move off and glanced at the marshal's stern face. "Have you got an idea where to look for Idaho Towner, Roman?" he asked directly.

The lawman shrugged. "Can't say I know any more than you do about this range. Might be able to track him away from here," he hazarded without enthusiasm. "That is, if I can pick up his sign—"

"We found where he hid his pony in the scrub the other night—over yonder." Pointing the spot out, Pat held Roman in talk while Sam piled the fresh supply of provisions on the porch. Ez and Kit came back presently with the pack horse. Although far from young, it was at least mild of manner and would probably be satisfactory. Stevens kept an eye on the proceedings until the packs were ready to be lashed down.

"Come on, Roman." He started down off the steps. "I'll show you where Towner started from, anyway. We didn't try trailing him ourselves, but you may have luck."

Out of the corner of his eye, Sam watched them start around the building. Waiting till they were well out of sight, he caught Ezra's attention and nodded significantly toward Kit.

"Get the horses, Ez."

Desultorily helping them pack, Majors paid no heed till he noted that the lanky tracker had led forward his own mount. His eyes widened in surprise. "What's that for?"

"You're going with us, boy." Sloan calmly moved up behind him to cut off his retreat. "Climb aboard that bronc."

Staring incredulously, Kit did not move. "You're crazy! You heard Roman say he's holding me. Are you trying to get me in worse trouble with him, or what?"

"Never mind. We'll square this deal with Roman," Ezra said dryly. "D'you think Stevens doesn't know what he's doing?"

Kit's eyes opened even wider. "Hold on! Is Stevens in on this?" He looked very much as if he wanted to draw back. "I don't owe that gent a thing—"

Bobby had been watching this from the store. Impulsively, she stepped out to the porch. "Go with them, Kit. Please," she begged. "I'm sure it's for the best."

But Kit remained balky. "You're just asking me to get myself in real trouble—"

Ez moved forward, stern resolution on his bleak face. "Will you climb onto that bronc, or will I throw you?"

Noting the very capable hand resting on Ezra's gaunt hip, Majors closed his lips tight and swung aboard.

"That's better." Ezra nodded. "Let's go—and just keep it in mind that we'll have an eye on you, boy, in case you get any ideas about quitting the bunch!"

6.

"YOU'VE got me in a real jam now," Majors protested as the store disappeared from sight. "If Roman comes flogging after us, I'll tell him how it happened!"

"You do that." Sam was short with him, while Ez said nothing at all. "Meanwhile just keep that bronc moving."

Kit did not make the mistake of hanging back, but it was plain he was anxious for Stevens to overtake them. He kept looking back as if dreading what he might see.

It was twenty minutes later, the trail behind them still empty, when Pat came riding calmly through the rocks from another direction. Majors searched his serene face for a clue to the future. Stevens only greeted him briefly.

"Glad you decided to come along," he remarked. "Maybe the four of us can get somewhere with those horses."

Kit realized that his kidnapping had been carefully planned beforehand. "Can you square this with the marshal, Stevens?" he challenged flatly.

Pat waved a hand. "I told him we'd keep an eye on you," he allowed.

"Why?"

Pat's curious glance lingered on Kit's face. "It doesn't seem to occur to you that Roman's got your safety in mind, as well as his own," he answered brusquely. "*He* knows you don't stand a chance with Towner, even if you don't."

Kit was incredulous and scornful. "So Roman is afraid I'll go after Idaho alone. Is that it?"

"Afraid for you." Pat cracked a frosty smile. "That's about it."

Majors retired into his private gloom. He made no trouble as the little party struck for the Uncompahgre, traveling steadily. It had been midday when they dropped down off the San Rafael hills; it was evening when they pulled up at a spring to make camp.

"You must know this range pretty well, boy," observed Pat as they sat about on the rocks eating supper. "Where would you go for prime stock?"

Kit gestured vaguely about. "Horses all around here," he muttered.

"I know that." Pat was patient. Pretending not to notice the other's depressed mood, he repeated his and Ezra's wholly unexpected experience with the mustangs. Kit came alert as he listened. It obviously heartened him to be treated as an equal by this competent man.

"You mean you're asking for my advice? . . . If it was me, Stevens, I'd pass up the scrub stuff around here," he said. "There's horseflesh over in the Breaks like you never saw before! But shucks—" He broke off dully. "What's the diff? Even Dad wouldn't listen to me!"

"Get this, kid! While you're one of this bunch and eating our grub, you'll pull your own weight," Ez yelled at him in simulated anger. "When we don't want your opinion we won't ask for it!"

Kit looked from one to the other. He was frankly bewildered. "You mean—I'm to help you fog the wild ones? I thought I was being dragged along to hold the horses," he blurted.

Sam laughed at him. "We're from Powder Valley, remember? This is your bailiwick, not ours. You'll get your full cut of whatever we pick up. If we're lucky, it might even set you up in business."

It was hard for Kit to realize that he was dealing with honest men who bore him no ill will. He broke out in a

sheepish grin. "Can I—count on all this, Stevens?" he
said uncertainly.

"I never intended anything else," Pat assured him.
"Just because I wouldn't step into a murder doesn't mean
I expect to take advantage of your hard luck."

With growing confidence, Majors leaned forward. "Just
so we understand each other. . . . The Breaks lay over
west another dozen or twenty miles, Stevens," he said
eagerly. "It's a wild, rugged piece of country, awful easy
to get lost in. You'll throw up your hands when you see it.
But there's horses there—good stock—the finest I ever
saw."

"Hard to get at, eh?" Sam drew him out tactfully.

"I got Dad in there just once," Kit said. "Horses all
around, and we never laid a rope on one. Pop was mad as
a hornet." He grinned.

Pat asked him to describe the Breaks. It was a vast area
of scattered canyons and knife-edged ridges, scarred and
cut up into incredible roughness. There was considerable
pine in the canyons; scattered springs and grama grass in
the secluded parks offered sanctuary to the mustangs.

"I've seen cougar in those crags, plenty of deer, and
even wild turkey in there," Kit went on. "You don't see
many shod tracks. But two men could spend a week in the
Breaks and never run into each other."

"Where else do the broomtails range?" pressed Ez.

"All over the Uncompahgre. The Breaks are only a
small part of it," Kit assured him. It did not take much
urging to start him relating a variety of horse-hunting
experiences. He told them the work was too strenuous to
pursue consistently; but valuable herds had come out of the
country, numbering into the thousands of animals, and it
was loosely estimated that probably another ten thousand
remained.

"Wild horse heaven!" Sam exclaimed with manifest
satisfaction. "We'll try these Breaks Majors is telling
about. The four of us ought to corner a decent bunch in
there."

They rolled up in their blankets, and a vast silence

spread under the glittering stars. In the small hours a dull clatter of hoofs and a blast of equine alarm awakened them. Sloan dug his Colt out from under his saddle and fired two shots into the air. They heard the swiftly receding thud of wild horses.

"Hanged if they ain't come hunting *us*," Ez said in wonderment. "Question is: are they after water, or trying to toll our critters off?"

Without a reply, Sam stamped into his boots and stumbled off into the gloom. He was back shortly. "Must be one of their springs," he announced. "Our broncs are all right. Blame lucky we staked 'em out though."

Except for a distant wolf howl, the rest of the night passed quietly. They were astir at the crack of dawn. Young Kit was as eager as any at the prospect of penetrating the Breaks; and yet, following a hurried breakfast, he stood for a long moment, one foot in the stirrup, gazing over his pony's back toward the dun swell of the San Rafaels.

"Come on, Majors! Shake a leg," called Sam.

Instead of answering, Kit turned a gloomy look on Stevens. "I can't help thinking about Bobby Durgen and old Ducks back there. We all know what they're up against—"

"I'll relieve your mind," Pat said kindly. "Ed Roman said he'd be working out of Durgen's place for a spell. Towner won't be anxious to get close to him, if he's around at all."

Much relieved, Kit said gratefully, "You do think of things, don't you, Stevens?" He didn't refer again that day to his own troubles.

They set off without further delay, Majors in the lead occasionally indicating their direction with a wave. There was no question of their keeping a watch on him now, whatever the U.S. marshal thought of Kit's intentions. Reconciling himself readily to the rough-barked partners and obviously respecting Stevens, he became one of the party, sharing fully in their plans and expectations.

The sun was still high when they reached what Majors

said was the edge of the Breaks. From a low gap they looked out over a widespread area, a ragged basin miles in extent, its floor gashed and seamed in a hundred directions and studded by low peaks.

It did not look like horse country. But as they gazed, Ezra pointed out several birds circling over the crags. "Buzzards. They must be expecting dinner at some lion kill."

Once they started down into the Breaks, all sense of open space faded, the crumbling walls and rough buttes closing in about them. Pines massed halfway up the canyon slopes; dense brush often cluttered the gulches; there were areas of naked rock.

Pat glanced about sharply. "I suppose you know your way in here," he remarked to Majors. "But how can a man stalk horses in here without stumbling smack into them?"

Kit grinned. "You'll do that too. But climb a ridge like the lions do," he explained, "and you'll see quite a lot. That's how I caught on."

As it happened, they did hear a band of mustangs in early afternoon clattering down-canyon on the other side of a rocky dyke. Before they could clamber up for a look, however, the wild ones had fled from sight beyond a bend.

"They don't leave much sign on the rocks," commented Ezra, climbing down for a look. "We can see the tracks better down where the canyon opens out." As he said, they could read the tracks plainly later. Ez counted only a dozen or fifteen head in the bunch.

Kit was not much interested. "Plenty of small bands drifting around," he told them. "We'll run into better stuff. Might as well try for a fair-sized haul."

Stevens saw his point as the unusually rough character of the Breaks became increasingly more apparent. Bronc-hunting in this endless expanse of rocks, downed timber, and tortuous gullies would be no snap, whatever the reward.

In midafternoon Majors drew up in a rocky hollow. "I've been here before." He pointed ahead. "You can see over into two or three canyons from that ridge. But you have to leave the horses and climb.''

Riding as far as they could, they dismounted in a clump of pine and toiled upward. It was hot work. The sun beat down, and what little breeze there had been was cut off. Ezra was the first to reach the top, loose gravel rattling down behind him. "Hey! Quite a view from up here!" he called.

The others joined him, puffing. They seemed to have climbed to a region of crags, isolated heights surrounding them on all sides, near and far. Abysses of space separated these looming promontories. As Majors had promised, it was possible to gaze down through the narrow gaps into three different canyons.

"Look down there." It was Pat who spoke, pointing.

Dwarfed at this distance, no less than fifty or sixty wild horses were to be seen grazing quietly on the floor of the largest canyon.

Sloan unconsciously gripped Ezra's forearm. "Man! There's some prime studs in that bunch," he breathed.

"Quit it, will you?" Ez shook his grip off. "I ain't one of 'em—"

After the first look, Stevens spoke quietly. "Step back, boys. Those wild hawks can spot us in a hurry." They sank down behind a fringe of brush, kneeling on the crumbling shale while they talked it over.

"That band is worth a good try," Pat said. "But we'll have to out-think them, starting now. . . . Any box canyon or pocket around here that you know of, Majors?"

Kit shook his head. "They can leave that canyon by five or six different trails," he informed them. "They must know this country better than I ever will."

Pat made his decision with characteristic promptness. "All right. We'll have to drift them out of there as quietly as possible. Might be possible to haze them into an area where they're less familiar. Then it's a case of being lucky. We've no time for any wing-trap business, but I believe it would pay to build one in here at that." He

turned away, starting to climb down. "Let's clear out of
here before they wind us."

Delaying another moment to study the canyon briefly,
they crawled back below the crest, then rose and started
the descent. Within ten minutes they were back with the
ponies. They had to follow a twisting gulch around the far
end of the ridge and negotiate a windfall before they
approached the canyon in which the mustangs grazed.
Finally Pat pulled up.

"This'll do. Drift across the canyon, Ez, and let them
scent you. That'll start them moving."

They waited while the tall tracker pushed on. After a
while, there came to their ears the faint rumble of many
hoofs. Pat waved Sam and Majors forward. By the time
they joined Ez in the canyon, the mustangs were gone.
Stevens was content, however.

"We'll keep them on the move," he announced, as he
scanned the sky. "Three or four hours till sundown. . . .
We'll track the bunch as far as we can and pick up their
sign in the morning. Another day should see them begin to
tire."

They sighted the big herd once as they traveled, far up a
long stretch of canyon. They were deep in the wild Breaks
by sunset. There was no point in trying to push on in the
gloom, for they might inadvertently crowd and scatter the
herd, so they pulled up and camped.

At dawn they were off once more, with Ezra reading
trail. It was several hours before the tracks grew fresh; the
mustangs had drifted and grazed during the night. Stevens
ascended a low peak while the others waited, and studied
the corrugated terrain. He came sliding back down in
haste.

"Keep pushing them," he called. "Nothing that looks
like a blind canyon around here."

Late in the afternoon, sensing the mustangs were tiring,
Pat had another look from a high ridge. Two miles away,
the wild ones were following the base of a long, open
slant. They were in no haste. Here and there a mustang

paused to tear at a tuft of grass. Pat gauged the throw of the land and waved the others forward.

"The bunch will stop to graze if we let them," he pointed out. "Look up along the top of that open slant. A perfect hollow in the hills. . . . If we string out along this side of the ridge here, stretch our line out a half-mile opposite them, and show ourselves at the right time, they ought to turn straight up that slope. Close in behind them fast enough, and they're cornered."

Sam readily approved this plan, his beady black eyes still feasting on the horses below. "Some mighty prime animals there," he averred. "It looks like we stand to turn a pretty penny, Stevens."

"Spread out, boys." Pat directed them to their posts along the ridge. "Watch for my signal, and we'll all show ourselves at once. We can fire a shot or two if they don't head in the right direction. Hustle now!"

Abandoning the pack pony to fend for itself till the issue was decided, they strung out along the ridge, keeping well back out of sight. Pat followed their progress, keeping an eye on the mustangs at the same time. This was a ticklish maneuver. But one after another, Ezra, Sam and young Majors signaled their readiness with a wave.

When the time was right, Stevens whipped off his kerchief and waved it high. In unison with the others, he urged his bronc up to the crest of the ridge full in the open. He was about to spur on over and down, closing in behind the mustangs without an instant's delay, when a cry from Ezra halted him sharply.

Looking downward, Pat saw what had awakened the tall tracker's wrath. To his amazed consternation, three horsemen came riding boldly up the floor of the canyon, cutting directly across their carefully planned line of attack. The mustangs scented them and saw them an instant later. The shrill blast of a whistle came floating up. Almost instantaneously the wild band took flight, skimming away like windblown leaves and heading straight back down the canyon.

The four men on the ridge could only sit their mounts

atop the ridge and watch. Headed in their present direction
as they raced away before the interlopers, the mustangs
showed no intention whatever of climbing the slope where
a catch would be possible. There was nothing to halt their
flight for miles; with their wild love of freedom and hatred
of men they would not stop short of killing themselves.

Clearly, the trio who had ridden so inopportunely into
the scene were deeply excited by the racing herd. Yelling
and waving ropes, they dashed after in vain pursuit.

Pat was startled by Sam Sloan's angry voice. "Did you
spot that big hombre in the lead, Stevens? Recognize him,
don't you? It was Idaho Towner and no mistake about it!"

Pat's lips closed in a thin, determined line. "This time
Idaho barged into our affairs once too often," he muttered
grimly. As Kit and Ez came pounding forward, something
in Ezra's manner arrested Pat's attention. "What's wrong
now, Ez?"

"Had my troubles keeping this squirt Majors from rushing down there to tangle with Towner," growled the lanky
man.

Pat's nod was curt. "I know exactly how he feels.
Well," he said wearily, "I guess we'd better get out of
here."

7.

"WHAT does that mean? Stevens, you can't be giving it up—!" exclaimed Majors.

"Can't I?" Pat took the query literally. All his urgency had dropped from him. He waved toward the canyon. "Take a look. Nothing down there now but dust! And with one more ten-mile run in these horses, where would we get?"

Struck silent, they watched him turn deliberately back. Kit looked ready to make an angry outburst, but somehow he checked it. Meeting the young puncher's smoking gaze, Pat said, "Pick up that pack animal, will you, Majors, and we'll be on our way." There was a bite in his tone. Delaying momentarily, Kit shrugged and did as he was told.

It was a gloomy party that wound down into the canyon, making no pretense of haste, and set off on the back trail. Ezra and Sam hung back, reading the signs and muttering between themselves.

"There's their tracks—" Ez indicated the gouging hoof-prints left by Towner and his confederates. "You reckon they spotted us and done this on purpose?"

Sam shrugged. "It's like Idaho. *He* wouldn't have a chance, chousing them mustangs around. If he wanted to spoil it for us, he couldn't have done it better."

They saw that the renegades had clung to the trail for a matter of miles, drawing no closer to the wild horses but refusing to give up. Ezra's wrath increased. "They act like they were doing this for fun. By gorry, if it was me, I'd make 'em laugh on the other side.''

"Come on, you two," Pat called back impatiently. "No point stalling along."

They could not figure Stevens out, but they urged their ponies forward, nonetheless. "Huh! He ain't going no-where—why's he in such a sweat to get there?" grumbled Sam.

The tracks of the mustang band and the renegades swung off into a side canyon, but Pat did not alter his determined course. When they camped at dusk beside a spring, dis-gruntled feelings held them all silent. During the night a rush of hoofs over the rocks told of mustangs scared away from the water. Later, an unearthly scream echoing in the crags jerked them upright in their blankets.

"What was that?" Majors gasped.

"Cougar," returned Ez. "Don't hear it often. I've known a man to spend years in lion country and never hear one."

Making sure their own horses were safe, they settled down. It seemed only minutes before dawn came stealing across the ridges. That morning they won out of the Breaks by steady travel, and afternoon saw them approaching the San Rafaels.

The partners had long since realized that Stevens was heading straight for Durgen's store. They took it for granted he was giving up the whole project as impractical. While it was true that Idaho Towner had ruined several days' work for them, they thoroughly disapproved of letting the man get away with it.

As for young Kit, he seemed to have lost all interest in the trio. It was plain that he was accompanying them to Durgen's only out of stubborn curiosity. Even if Stevens had given up, he could still hope that Marshal Roman might show interest in the outlaw's whereabouts.

The isolated store looked as deserted as ever when they drew near an hour before sunset. A saddle horse stood switching at flies, and after looking it over briefly, Pat dismounted to make directly for the store door. The others were close behind him.

Ed Roman stood at the counter in conversation with Bobby Durgen. He turned to scrutinize them in his usual methodical manner. "Came back, did you, Stevens?" he inquired laconically.

Pat assented. "I wanted to get here while you were still around, Roman." He paused while everyone waited in suspense for his next words. "I've decided I'll take on that job of running down Idaho Towner."

For a moment, utter silence greeted his announcement. Kit's look was one of blank amazement. Ezra was the first to voice his feelings. "If that's the case, why didn't you make up that thing you call your mind while we still had Towner in sight?" he exploded.

Roman looked startled. "Don't tell me you ran into Idaho out there?" he barked.

"Well—let's say he ran into us." Imperturbably, Pat described how Towner and two companions had ruined their chance with the mustangs so smoothly as to make it appear deliberate. "I don't know if it was planned or not. But Idaho wouldn't have cared—and I've had enough. We'll never be left free to run horses till he's been brought to account," he said flatly. "I'll carry your badge, Roman, and go after that blackleg on one condition—"

"What's that?" Roman was suspicious.

"You asked me to tackle this," Pat reminded him bluntly. "Experience warns me there's usually a half-dozen strings attached. This time I insist on doing it my own way, or I'm still not interested. Do I make myself clear?"

The federal marshal gave no indication of being influenced one way or the other. "How *will* you do it, Stevens?"

Pat spread a hand, palm down. "That," he retorted coolly, "is the one condition. You want Idaho Towner—I'll undertake to hand him over to you. But I want a free hand, Roman. I'll tell you how it was done after it's over." His pause was significant. "Take it or leave it."

The lawman grunted. "Hard man to deal with, ain't you?" But he did not sound overly annoyed. "I've watched your work in the past, Stevens. Results are what I want—

and I can't complain about you there." He pulled a badge out of his pocket. "Hold up your hand."

"Wait a minute." Pat stepped back before he could pin the badge on. "You've said everything except whether you'll accept my conditions or not. I'm not after the honor, Roman. I needn't tell you it'll be all hard work. Which will it be—yes or no?"

Ed Roman did look faintly irritated at last. "Giving you the job, ain't I?" he r‚ped. "Don't be so blamed picky, man!"

For answer, Pat started to turn abruptly toward the door. "Nothing more for us here." He waved the partners that way, ignoring the look of alarmed dismay which passed between young Majors and the girl.

"All right—wait a minute now. Dang it, have it your own way, Stevens," Roman interposed hastily. "I'll agree to anything short of bribery! Towner will have a tough time with you if you're as touchy as this with me."

"That's more like it." Now Pat allowed him to pin on the deputy's badge. Roman made sure it was fastened and stepped back.

"Repeat after me . . ." He swore Pat in, and after it was over, stood looking at him in some puzzlement. "Now what? Are you taking these old rawhides with you, Stevens?"

Ez and Sam promptly bristled. "Rawhide yourself, Roman!" snarled the former. "Afraid you'll have to pay us too, or wnat?"

Pat calmly ignored the question. "I'll notify you when I'm ready to turn Towner over," he said civilly. "If you're not here, better leave word where you can be reached, just in case."

"I'm used to knowing what my deputies are up to," the lawman stated crustily. "Just don't rush off is all I ask. If you should grab Idaho," he explained, "there's people I want notified at once."

"How come, Roman?" Sam put in brazenly. "Is there a reward attached to that hombre?"

It suited the marshal to answer without hesitation.

"Twenty-five hundred," he said. "I thought Stevens understood that. Makes it worthwhile to drop horse hunting for a while, don't it?" He sounded as if he thought this argument irresistible.

"Lay off, Marshal!" Kit sounded bitter. "My Dad's murder is at stake here. The dirty dollars don't matter."

"Ought to." The lawman was blunt. "Some of them dollars will give you a fresh start, boy. And from what I hear, you can use it."

Paying no heed to this exchange, Pat instructed Ezra to replenish their supplies. Sam grain-fed the horses, busying himself in preparation for a fresh start. Getting no satisfaction from Roman, Kit turned away and stepped in through the rear for a word with Ducks Durgen.

It was then that Ed Roman drew Stevens aside, making sure they were by themselves. "I'm not bothered about you, Stevens—but this time we'll have to make other arrangements for young Majors."

Pat's response was dry. "You asked me to watch the boy before."

"I know. But I can't afford no deputy just to keep an eye on him," Roman spoke plainly. "He's hot after Towner's scalp—and I want Idaho brought in alive."

Pat knew the argument was just. Kit Majors was levelheaded for his age, but he had proved himself impulsive; and Stevens was forced to admit the puncher had unusual provocation. He nodded. "I'll see that he stays behind."

The lawman glanced at him shrewdly. "Like to do things your way, don't you, Stevens? But I expect your word'll do."

Nevertheless, he delayed to watch Pat's first moves. With Ez and Sam busily occupied, it was not long before all was in readiness. Only then did Kit emerge from his talk with Durgen. Bobby lay in wait for him, however, in the store and held him still longer. From the tone of their raised voices, it could be surmised that the puncher was not only declining to inform Bobby of his intentions, but that he was anxious to break away.

Pat was waiting for him as he burst out of the door.
"Where away, Majors?" he called out directly.

Kit looked up, surprised. "I'm going with you," he
brought out unguardedly.

Pat shook his head. "Sorry. We may have to stretch
those supplies a long ways. Afraid there won't be room for
an extra man this trip."

Kit clattered down the porch steps and came striding
forward. "But look here! You can't leave me behind now.
You're going after Idaho Towner, and I'm going with you.
Nothing will stop me till that wolf has been run down and
wiped out!"

Pat put up an arresting hand. "Wait a minute. I know
exactly how you feel about him. But, Majors, if you think
anything at all of Bobby Durgen, you'll want to watch her
closer than you'll be able to do if you go with us."

Pat's words gave Kit pause. Yet he was not wholly
persuaded. "What are you driving at now—?"

Pat lowered his voice. "Don't let it get to her. But
Towner will finish her off quick as an only witness if he
sees the situation tightening up. You've seen how fast he
moves. You simply can't afford to take a chance with him,
boy."

"Nonsense!" Kit scoffed. "Don't you get it, Stevens?
With me along, we'll keep him on the run so tight he
won't know what's happening until it's all over."

Pat's smile had little mirth in it. "I used to figure that
way—at your age. We're going after Towner, sure. It
doesn't seem to occur to you that he could hang *our* hides
on the fence." His lips were a thin line. "That makes a
difference, doesn't it? You've found out already that you
don't win every time."

Kit looked half persuaded, but he wouldn't give in yet.
"This is all foolishness," he burst out. "Why don't we all
go—Roman too? Tough as he is, Idaho Towner can't buck
the army! I aim to have this over with fast—"

Pat stared at him coldly. "Telling me my business now,
are you? I made Roman agree to let me handle this my
way, and I won't change that for you. Leave that girl here

alone, Majors, and I won't answer for her life. So make up your mind!''

Kit whirled toward Roman. "You're not going along with Stevens," he challenged him. "Won't you be here?"

Roman appeared to be waiting for this. "No," he said with an edge to his tone. "For that matter, I haven't come to a decision yet about you. You ought to be hauled along and tucked in a safe place. I don't like a man that's too free with his lead—and I haven't forgotten my introduction to you."

Kit immediately looked chagrined. "I'll stay here," he muttered. "If the marshal won't do it, somebody's got to! But I only hope you drive that rat this way, Stevens," he could not keep himself from adding.

Pat played the pretense out. "Will that be okay, Roman?"

"I reckon," Ed conceded grudgingly. "Long as he undertakes to keep out of the way while we do our work."

The lawman's word reduced the puncher to something like helpless desperation. Turning away with an exclamation, he slammed up the plank steps and into the store. Pat made an opportunity later to step inside for tobacco.

"Don't forget, Majors," he spoke up for the girl's benefit. "We'll want a close watch on Towner or any of his pals around here. I'll expect a careful report later of anything you happen to see."

Bobby smiled at Pat gratefully. "I'm sure he'll be able to tell you anything worth hearing about. It'll be a relief to know he's here to help us."

If that cheered Kit at all, he failed to show it, and he neither evinced any further interest in Roman's movements nor came to the door to watch the departure of the Powder Valley trio a few minutes later. The girl lifted a hand to them from the porch while the federal officer stood by.

"Pat, there's really nothing to prevent your staying overnight, and your horses can stand the rest," called Bobby, although she did not really expect an affirmative answer.

"No, we'll shove along a mile or two and camp," Pat

returned quietly. "Roman can tell you it's worth our while to pick up a warm trail."

No more was said until the Durgen establishment dropped out of sight to the rear. Then, Sam turned to Stevens. "You don't honestly expect to pick up Towner's sign where we last saw it?" he demanded.

"I had to say something," Pat explained. "We got Majors off our hands, and I don't fancy Ed Roman around giving orders, for that matter. Or do you want him to hold your hand?" he ended derisively.

Sloan subsided into hurt silence. Ezra's grin at his discomfiture faded into frowning thought. "You must have some scheme or other," he hazarded. "How *will* we go about laying this buzzard by the heels, Stevens?"

"That should work itself out. One advantage we have over Towner is that he never saw us before. That ought to be useful to us—"

"You mean walk right up on him?" Sam was jarred into curiosity.

Pat shrugged. "I doubt if anybody can do that, wary as he knows he's got to be. Too long a chance."

"Give it to us then," Ez demanded. "You must have some scheme worked out."

"Why, Roman handed it to us himself. He picked up the rumor that Towner's hiding out with the horse hunters; and from what we've seen, he's right." Pat looked from one to the other, watching their response. "We'll *join* those horse hunters ourselves and watch our luck," he went on. "It won't be easy. Ten to one, Idaho isn't with them much of the time. But that's our best chance."

Ezra was weighing this. "I don't know . . . What if those horse hunters turn out to be real chummy with Towner?" he queried keenly.

"There's that to consider," Pat agreed coolly. "We'll have time to figure it out while we're waiting for him to show up. And if you're right and they are a part of his gang, we'll know exactly what we're up against—and we'll just have to tough it out."

8.

DRIVING deep in wild, strange country the following day, they needed no reminder that this was wild horse range. If they saw less than usual of the mustangs, the signs of their presence were everywhere.

Not once during the day, however, did they glimpse a human being or so much as the print of a shod hoof. Pat was undisturbed by this. "Somewhere there must be places where it's easier to catch the wild ones," he opined. "That's where the hunters will be."

About them in every direction stretched the unbroken emptiness and silence typical of unexplored country. Yet Sam professed the uncanny feeling of being watched.

"That could be," Ez said grimly. "With horses *and* owlhoots around—none of 'em blind."

"Just remember we're supposed to be hunting broncs," Pat advised. "If anyone should be watching us, that's the impression we want them to get."

If a watcher was keeping tabs on them during the long afternoon, there was no visible sign of it. They camped at sunset on a bench overlooking miles of unbroken wilderness, and before the light failed, they saw a band of mustangs straggling across the far shoulder of a butte.

Setting out at dawn the next day, they began to watch for mustangs in earnest. As it turned out, they had not long to wait. At Ezra's suggestion, shortly after sunrise they waited for an hour at a rocky waterhole.

Not much to their surprise, a band of eighteen or twenty

wild horses clattered in for water. Reined up behind a granite dyke, the trio delayed long enough to examine the animals with some care. A large share of the bunch proved stunted and runty, but two or three were good enough to draw a grunt of approval from Sloan.

"Shall we rush 'em and see how they act?" he muttered.

Having had a careful look, Pat nodded. Most of the wild ones were gathered near the catch basin, grouped on the apron of sheet rock surrounding the spot. Tails switching and wild heads held erect and alert, they waited their turn at the water. A sage-laden breeze blowing down from the heights prevented them from scenting the humans near at hand.

Quickly the three got set. Ez raised a bony hand, peering cautiously out at the quarry. He signaled sharply, and they roweled their mounts from cover, dashing madly toward the mustangs. For a few brief seconds pandemonium reigned. Fierce squeals and whistles rang out as the untamed brutes strove to escape. One or two plunged straight up the rocks with goatlike agility; several lost their footing and crashed down, throwing the others into confusion as they struggled up.

Swinging lariats and yelling harshly to further rattle the animals, the trio closed in with a rush. Sam missed his cast at a valuable horse which dodged and lunged away; cursing excitedly, he sought to retrieve his rope. Ezra was luckier, his loop settling around the neck of a salty two-year-old.

Before there was time for any second guesses the band scattered, racing away in a dozen directions. It would have been wasted effort to pursue them over the treacherous ground. Sloan turned, scowling, to look at the scrawny broomtail Stevens had snagged. "Ain't got much of an eye for horses, have you?"

Pat's laugh was rueful. "These babies are smart," he admitted. "The big roan I had an eye on sure must have known it! He made one fast move, and before *I* knew it, my rope was on this thing." He was not certain himself exactly how it had happened.

Ez gave them both a scornful glance. He was busy mastering the glossy two-year-old. "We keeping these dogs?" he demanded.

"We can take along that one you got for the looks of it," Pat tossed back. "I've seen worse, if I wouldn't come this far to pick it up." He laughed again. "Help me tie loose from this bearcat, Sam."

It took their combined efforts to get Pat's rope off the panicked broomtail. Once free the animal fled without a backward look for its unfortunate companion.

"Bring up that pack pony," Ezra ordered. "We'll tie this critter on a long lead and haze it along a while till it gets the idea."

For a time, the wild captive bade fair to break the pack pony's legs or neck, dragging it across the rocks. The men worked with it patiently, until at length sheer exhaustion induced a measure of docility.

During the afternoon, they saw several other mustang bands. A surprising number of the animals were excellent stock.

"We could make a haul right around here, Stevens," Ez speculated. "Build a rock corral in some gully and toss the stuff in as we catch it. I'd undertake to catch that roan herd we was after in two weeks—"

Pat did not appear to hear him. "On this kind of range, it can't be long before we stumble across that camp," he mused. "Keep an eye peeled for shod tracks, both of you."

They failed to run across the sign they sought, but later in the afternoon, Sam did spot a distant horseman. He called his discovery to the attention of the others. Drawn up on a ridge, they watched the progress of the stranger. Whether he saw them or not, within minutes the solitary rider changed his direction and appeared to be drawing steadily away from them.

Stevens nodded to himself. Far from being annoyed, he seemed to take cheer from the incident. "The hunters are around," he declared. "It's only a matter of time now. We don't want to seem anxious anyway."

On the following day, they spotted another rider, who this time deliberately turned back. Later Ez found the tracks of several shod ponies. Ten minutes' study told them they were within the area in which the horse hunters were working. That afternoon, pretending not to know they were being watched, they took pains to be seen chasing a stray band of broomtails. They made no effort to conceal either their camping place or their cooking fire that night.

On the following morning, however, Ezra dropped all pretense of watching for horses. "Reckon I can take us straight to that horse camp now," he proposed.

Pat accepted this calmly. "No sweat about it. If we get there along toward dark, the men will all be in."

Late afternoon found them working toward the mouth of a secluded canyon, following numerous shod tracks. A half-mile from its craggy gateway, Stevens dismounted and pried a shoe from one of his pony's hoofs. The partners watched this, exchanging a knowing and appreciative glance.

Keeping to the open, they pushed on. A thin skein of woodsmoke showed through the pines once they got inside the entrance to the canyon. Ez had detected it ten minutes before. Presently a harsh male voice rang out from beyond the fringe of scrub saplings, and another answered.

They rode through a gap in the pines into a grassy open space. Here, under the trees, the wild-horse hunters had established their camp. Over three small fires, men squatted in the evening light cooking their supper. There was even a rude camp wagon here, its box piled with bedrolls.

The rough voices died out abruptly at their appearance. A brawny, bearded man rose deliberately, gave them a good once over, and came forward without haste.

Pat held up a hand in greeting. "Smelled your smoke just now and dropped by to say howdy," were his opening words. "I'm Pat Stevens, and this is Sam and Ezra."

The big man nodded, studying them with veiled curiosity. "Gabe Marsh is my name," he supplied. It was apparent he was the acknowledged head of the horse hunters. "Any luck?" he pursued gruffly, his eyes on the lone mustang trailing a rope's length behind the pack pony.

"Not much." Pat allowed faint chagrin to color his tone. "I was wondering if you could spare a few nails, Marsh? My bronc threw a shoe—"

Still in no hurry, Marsh signed his assent. "Might as well haul up now you're here," he said. "I expect you can all use a bait of grub."

Well aware that it was not good manners under any circumstances to show undue curiosity in a strange camp, it was all they could do to keep from raking the entire place with wary eyes. Not till all had been fed, however, were they able to ascertain that Idaho Towner was nowhere about at the moment. It was probably this fact—if Towner came here at all—that accounted for Gabe Marsh's ready welcome.

After the meal, Marsh came over to where they sat cross-legged before the fire. Rolling a smoke, he gazed thoughtfully into the dusk before speaking. "Mustang-running your regular trade, Stevens?" he opened up casually.

"No." Pat had removed the law badge and stowed it in a pocket soon after Ed Roman had sworn him in. "At least, it's been quite a while, and we're a little rusty. But a man's got to make a dollar somehow."

The words drew a familiar picture of drifting range men, weary of riding from ranch to ranch and job to job. Moving forward silently to listen, the horse hunters could understand this talk, a little experience having brought them here themselves. Looking them over, Pat found them a rough and hearty lot, perhaps not overly bright but honest enough as such groups went.

"That's so." Marsh neither approved nor doubted. His critical eye strayed over their outfit, fitting their words to their condition. "A man can pick up a living here in the Uncompahgre if he knows how—"

"Wrong season right now," Ez remarked.

"Yes." The bearded leader agreed gravely. "Too much water in the holes. But later, in the dry season, the mustangs drift north into the mountains—so it's all one."

"They're never easy to snag, that's a fact," admitted Pat with a laugh. He glanced ruefully at the single broomtail they had brought along. "We hope to do better."

There was more talk of range conditions. Marsh was careful to point out the boundaries of the general area he and his men were working.

"That's okay." It was Sam who responded, apparently unaware the hunters were alertly awaiting the answer. "We want our own hunting country too. Plenty of room around for all. But Stevens needed those nails," he reminded them.

Their jealous curiosity somewhat satisfied, the horse hunters began to make final arrangements for the night. It was taken for granted that the trio would camp in the canyon. But big Gabe was careful to make one point in his casual talk.

"Don't go far up-canyon, Stevens, if you move around," he advised.

"Corral up that way, eh?" Pat caught Gabe's warning. "And thanks for the nails, Marsh. We'll probably be gone early."

Moving a hundred yards off from the hunters, the three built their own small fire. Pat heated the iron shoe and tacked it on, while Sam and Ezra made camp. Knowing that Marsh would post a routine guard or two, they rolled up in their blankets, expecting an undisturbed sleep.

Pat was the first awake in the morning. A horse hunter or two was already astir in the other camp. Ignoring them, the three were up and away before full daylight. Ez looked back more than once as they left the shadowy canyon. Finally he spoke. "I thought you aimed to join that bunch, Stevens?" he challenged.

"Let's not rush matters, shall we?" Pat said with a grin. "At least we know Towner's not around—and I don't want Marsh to get the idea we're anxious."

"So how do we work it?" asked Sam.

Pat shrugged. "Idaho will be back," he predicted. "We'll watch that crowd for a day or so and try to keep out of sight. At least we've got it fixed in Gabe Marsh's mind that it's horses we're interested in, if they do spot us."

Fortunately, the leader had indicated that his party was working north of the canyon. By giving their attention to the broken country lying to the south, they had some shadow of permission to remain fairly near the canyon.

After driving on far enough to make sure they were no longer observed, they spent an hour setting up a hidden camp at which to leave the pack pony and mustang. This done, they turned back.

Pat suggested that they separate, each seeking some point of vantage on high ground from which to watch the operations of the horse hunters. In late afternoon they met once more at their camp. Ezra's report was meager. He had seen nothing at all of particular interest.

"They're a hard-working bunch, I'll say that," Sloan reported. "They seem to hunt up these wild bunches, corner them and rope what they can. I expect with a catch of five or six head every day or so it mounts up." He had watched a group of the hunters chasing a band of mustangs for several hours, finally wearing them down and capturing two or three animals. "If you ask me, Stevens, they got nothing on their minds except horseflesh," he concluded.

Pat had come to the same conclusion. He had seen nothing to indicate that the hunters were aware of being watched, or would care particularly if they did know. "I don't suppose either of you saw anything of Idaho Towner—?"

Neither of them had.

Thinking it over as they ate supper, Pat worked out a plan. "We'll try it another day. I want another look at that canyon. And if we could make sure Idaho is going to be around before we hook up with that crowd, that would be swell. But I suppose we'll wind up fishing for information."

On the following day they continued their watch. Once Ezra was forced to ignore a mustang band he might easily have cornered, much to his disgust. This time he trailed the hunters, observing them from afar. His report in camp that night was succinct and final.

"We're wasting our time," he said flatly. "If there's one owlhoot hiding in Marsh's camp, the rest don't know it or don't care. They're harmless, hard-working fools, Stevens—and so are we."

This blunt judgment settled matters for Pat. "We'll shove on back there tomorrow," he decided. "This time we'll try our luck another way."

Late afternoon of the following day saw them filing wearily into the secluded canyon once more. They had seen to it that the ponies wore a dusty, tired look, and their own manner was one of dejected defeat.

"Back again, eh?" big Gabe greeted them gruffly without surprise. "Grab a bait, boys. You look like you could use some rest!"

This time the looks thrown their way were faintly hostile, and the hunters supplied them with food very grudgingly. The whole atmosphere of the camp seemed charged with suspicion, in sharp contrast to their first visit.

Marsh scarcely waited to finish eating before accosting them directly. "No luck, I take it?" he asked offhandedly.

Pat's headshake expressed discouragement. "We missed out on a grand catch, Marsh. This just isn't the kind of country two or three men can work to advantage. We've run our broncs' legs off and got nowhere."

Gabe shrugged. "Horse hunting never was easy." His men had now gathered around to listen.

"The mustangs are here," Pat proceeded doggedly. "I've watched a fortune run past the end of my rope. The right method is to have plenty of hands—as you seem to have found out."

Gabe failed to answer at once, eyeing them dourly. Pat threw him a straight glance, and made a blunt proposal. "We're asking if we can join up with your crowd, Marsh."

This evoked a buzzing murmur among the horse hunters. Before any direct response could be given, there was a stir on the edge of the group, and a big man thrust his way through. "What's all this?" he rasped. "Who are these pushy birds, Gabe?"

Pat and his friends found themselves looking into the scowling face of Idaho Towner.

9.

THE three men looked up blankly at the burly renegade, as if they found no significance beyond the moment in his sudden appearance, and turned back to Marsh.

"Who are they?" Gabe's dry tone revealed his dislike of Towner. "They're horse hunters, Idaho—like the rest of us."

"Why ain't they out crowding the broomtails then?" growled Idaho. "There's nothing around here for them."

Marsh explained that the three men had found it impossible to work effectively by themselves. "Reckon you know how that is yourself," he added.

"Nothing doing," Towner broke in before Gabe finished speaking. "Don't get bighearted! If they're clumsy enough to fumble a mustang catch, why give 'em ours?" He glowered at the newcomers. "Send them packing, Gabe!"

At least one or two muttering voices approved Towner's stand. Others waited for a response from Marsh. Instead of voicing a final decision, Gabe shot a questioning glance at Pat.

"There's one vote against you, Stevens—"

Pat offered no vigorous protest. "Oh well. I didn't know this gent was your boss," he said smoothly. "We didn't run into him the first time."

That jarred Gabe. No less than Pat and the partners, he was keenly aware of a rising rumble from the majority of his men. "He's not," he snapped. "Whatever he thinks!"

72

His pause was deliberate. "Fact is, we *can* use more hands. I think we'll give you and your friends a try, Stevens, if you'll be satisfied with wages—"

"Marsh, don't be a fool!" Towner rang out sharply. "You don't know who these hombres are. There's plenty of wanted men on the run looking for a nice soft spot and willing to let you do their fighting. You've put in a lot of work already, you and the boys. Don't get us all in trouble for three cheap drifters!'

Ignoring him, Marsh waited for Pat's response. The latter nodded reluctantly. "We'll take it," he said at last. "Wages are something anyway."

The big outlaw met this with a snarl of contempt. "You were warned, buster," he bawled at Marsh. "And that goes for these—"

"Hold on now, Towner." Big Gabe was slow to anger, but his wrath was stirred up by this show of open defiance. "What am I to take it you mean by this? Are you pulling out on us? . . . *You* came here and asked to join up. Maybe you're taking over my job now?"

"Don't want it." Idaho was striving to convey the impression that he could take over if he wanted to.

"That's nice to know." Marsh's sarcasm was stern. "And don't forget the rest of us are working while you're off riding around. Because we'll remember it too."

Towner stalked off, letting the matter drop here for the moment.

The episode cleared the air somewhat for Pat and the partners. Most of Gabe's men seemed grudgingly willing to defend them against Idaho's unwarranted attack, and there could be little doubt that they knew exactly what sort of man Towner was.

Pat made little of the situation. "We'll get along somehow," he assured Gabe.

Turning to business, Marsh revealed that, while the hunters had trapped a number of mustangs, progress was not altogether satisfactory, and they were seriously considering the construction of a large wing trap. The services of the trio would be more than welcome in such an extensive project.

Ez had already divined as much, watching the men ride to and fro the previous day as if seeking a logical site. "In the right place it'll pay off big," he spoke up. "And with enough hands, in this country you can make as many drives as you want."

"Any experience with wing traps?" asked Gabe keenly. When Ez gave a laughing assent, he nodded in satisfaction. "So have I—but I don't pretend to know all the wrinkles. We'll go over the scheme again in the morning, and we can get to work."

As before, the trio camped by themselves. Pat had only a murmured word or two for the others as he turned in. "Sleep light," he advised briefly. "I don't think Towner will try anything, but it'll pay to be ready for him."

After an uneventful night, Marsh and half-a-dozen men ate a hearty breakfast and then set out to re-examine the site tentatively selected for the horse trap. Pat and the partners went along. Seeing them start off, Idaho Towner hastily mounted and came jogging after the party. Gabe waited for him.

"What now, Idaho?"

"I'm going along," Towner said, suspiciously eyeing the others in the group. "Want to see what this trap will look like."

"Later." Marsh made it plain that he was not welcome on this occasion. "We'll use you all right once we get our plans laid."

The outlaw truculently thrust out his hard jaw. Before he answered, however, two rough-looking characters Pat had observed clinging close to Towner last night rode out to join him.

"Come on, Idaho," one called scornfully. "We know where to find the wild ones."

Towner hesitated, but finally turned back with a disgruntled air. Sam's lingering glance rested on the three as they rode away. "They any good at this game?" he wondered aloud.

Marsh's mouth hardened. "They're three more hands." His curt response seemed to close the subject.

An hour later Ez was able to point out the obvious disadvantages of the site the hunters had picked for the wing trap. There was argument, but these men were willing to listen to hard sense. Later Ez picked a spot they would never have considered, lying just over the brow of a low swell which overlooked the rocky canyon below.

"There's your trap," he said flatly.

Gabe Marsh gazed about the spot, frowning. "Why here?"

Ezra explained. "You can fog any number of mustangs up or down the canyon yonder," he said. "Spot a man or two in the canyon, when you make a run, below the trap. Once they show themselves, the mustangs'll take off up the slope here. This low gap is a natural pass—they'll make for it and be inside your trap wings and on into the corral before they know it."

Gabe saw the plan. Clearly, it appealed to him. "We may have to try more than once, but we'll try this first," he decided. "Plenty of cedar and such trash along the ridge here to work with. Rocks too. We'll pack the tools out here this afternoon and pitch in."

Idaho was conspicuously absent later when a dozen or more axes and mattocks were pulled out of the camp wagon. Pat saw Marsh looking about for him, but it was Ezra who spoke up. "Want me to locate that busy hombre?" he asked. "We can use his beef now." He looked eager to undertake such an assignment.

Gabe shook his head. "He knows we got work here," he returned. "He'll get his share before we finish."

If Towner knew, he conveniently forgot it for the balance of this day, breezily riding his sweat-stained bronc into camp before dusk, with his cronies trailing him as usual. They had made no catch, but that did not bother them. "We sure flogged them wild babies over the rocks," bragged Idaho, coolly helping himself to food prepared by others.

Every other man in camp had been laboriously grubbing

brush or rolling rocks at the new trap. Most of the glances tossed at the carefree trio were sullen. That little or nothing was said openly revealed the measure of the big outlaw's subtle domination of the hunters.

"Towner must get a boot out of exercising the broomies. He ain't nothing but an overgrown kid," growled Sam, eating at a nearby fire. "Wonder just who that pair with him is?"

"Small-time owlhoots, probably." Pat shrugged. A generous bite of venison halfway to his lips, he suddenly lowered his tone. "Watch this—"

Gabe Marsh was making his way toward Towner. A big man, he matched Idaho in size and imposing manner. "We started work on that trap, mister," he announced flatly. "I'll expect you there tomorrow—if you're working with us."

"Somebody's got to keep an eye on camp and put meat in the pot," Idaho blustered.

"Never mind. We had that out before." Gabe eyed him bleakly. "You heard me, Towner." He started to turn away.

"Oh, I'll do my part," Idaho assured him loftily.

"He doesn't know how right he is," muttered Ez. Ezra's words sounded like a promise, and he kept it the very next morning.

Towner had boisterously preceded everyone to the trap, racing out on his pony. Clearly, it was not his intention to take the work seriously. But Ez, with his knowledge of mustangs and the art of masking an altered landscape, had quietly taken charge of construction of the quarter-mile-long trap wings. He brusquely ordered Idaho to start rolling rocks into position.

"*Ha-ha-ha.*" Towner's scornful laugh was unconvincing. He sobered quickly, conscious of others watching. "It's against my principles to get off my horse," he remarked flippantly. "Roll your own rocks, old sport."

Ez refused to fool with him. "Marsh," he called. "Throw this tramp off the job. We need his beef on those rocks, but he's too good for hard work. Doesn't want to get his hands dirty!''

It took nerve to say this, considering the cold-blooded savagery they had seen Idaho display. The renegade's beefy face flamed. He was ready for violence.

Gabe came stumping forward. "Come on, Idaho. Get busy. We all have to pitch in." He was short with Towner.

Towner glared murderously at Ezra. If he hadn't known that Stevens and Sam Sloan were narrowly watching his every move, he might have thrown his gun. "Don't tell me this old rip is my boss," he rasped. "He may be *yours!*"

Marsh refused to take the bait. "Come on, come on. We're all after horses here. If you aren't, Towner, I guess that settles it."

Gabe's finality was too much for Idaho. He had no taste for being told to ride out of the horse camp and not to come back. Muttering angrily, he slowly dismounted.

Ez wouldn't let up on him. Towner was soon rolling and pushing huge rocks into position. Pat and Sam were in the midst of this work also. There was no denying that Towner's rugged brawn was an asset. He took a boastful pride in tumbling boulders the others could not budge. Before long it grew painfully apparent that he was deliberately trying to antagonize Stevens.

As they were thrusting shoulder to shoulder at a huge rock, Idaho got bossy. "Hang it all, give me room!" He tried to trip Pat, shoving him roughly aside.

Lips thin, Pat coolly stepped back. But for Towner's confederates hovering watchfully about, he could have laid Idaho out cold, taking him prisoner on the spot.

A moment later the big outlaw tried the same trick again. This time Pat's spike heel came down crushingly on his instep, jerking a bawl of pain out of him. In a killing passion, Idaho could only stagger aside nursing his numb foot, his venomous eyes blazing.

"Tough luck," Pat commiserated. "These accidents will happen. You seemed to get right under me."

Thereafter, Towner's hatred was blatant. But his actions

were more circumspect, and if Ezra bore down on him
without letup, he did not openly attempt to retaliate.

The work proceeded steadily. Slowly the wings length-
ened, with cut brush and saplings masking the rocky barri-
ers. Several men under Gabe's direction erected a stout
corral directly in the throat of the wings, and partially
concealed by rocks too large to move.

The men took a brief break at noontime to eat in the
scant shade. They were soon at work once more. In midafternoon Ez was riding back from a short trip out to the
brush-cutters when Cash Avery, who had been left on
guard at the camp in the canyon, came racing up the slope.

"There's hell to pay, Gabe!" he burst out. "A bear
threw a scare into those mustangs we're holding! They
busted down the corral fence, and they're rampaging all
over the canyon! Fisher's trying to hold 'em, but we need
help!"

Without a word, Ez wheeled his mount in the direction
of the canyon and raced off. Others dashed to follow suit.
Before they could saddle their grazing broncs, however,
Idaho and his two cronies grasped this opportunity to vault
astride their waiting ponies and pound away. Sam snorted
his disgust.

"I saw those buzzards never off-saddled here on the
job," he called to Pat. "But we didn't any of us expect
this!"

With a comparatively fresh horse, Ez meanwhile out-
distanced Avery on the way back to the canyon. He was
barely in time to turn back several magnificent and terri-
fied mustangs in the act of making a break for the open.
Hazing them up the canyon, he presently caught sight of
Fisher, the other guard.

"Watch yourself, Ezra," the grizzled oldtimer sang out.
"That bear's still after the broncs!"

"Keep 'em crowded back," Ez flung across. "I'll cruise
around and make short work of that critter!"

Leaving the open trail, he hurled his mount through
thick underbrush and thrust on under the pines. Sight was
not good in this maze, but he could depend on his pony to

signal the proximity of the invading killer. Within minutes Ez heard harsh voices calling out farther down canyon behind his position. More help was coming, but he did not pause. The sloping sides of the canyon were rough. The bronc stumbled over a rocky outcrop and lost some moments entangled in heavy brush.

The whistling blast of a mustang pierced the oppressive air of the canyon. Hauling up, Ez hearkened keenly. A faint, heavy crashing came to his ears from somewhere ahead. He started on—to rein down abruptly with iron hand as a vicious cry rang out.

"There he is—!"

Ezra's jaw tightened as he spotted Idaho Towner crashing toward him under the trees. One of his cohorts was in view farther on. Was it the bear they had seen, or him? A carbine cracked, and Ez felt rather than heard the flutter of the lethal slug past his face. He knew then. He was the quarry of this treacherous pair.

A scrape of rocks behind him revealed a third man and warned Ez unmistakably that the three were bent on cornering him against the canyon side. That they would shoot him down ruthlessly he did not question.

Rigidly mastering the spooky bronc under him, he thrust straight on in the direction of Towner. The thunderous clatter of racing mustangs farther out on the canyon floor did not distract his attention. Gun at the ready, Ez got a flash of Idaho and fired almost pointblank. Towner escaped the shot somehow, dodging behind scattered pine trunks.

"Here he is!" cried the outlaw piercingly "Close in on him—close in!"

Ez yelled a challenge. "Show yourself, you long-haired wolf! Let's get this over with!"

Towner's next shot clipped twigs over Ezra's head, and his rasping laugh sounded. "Nail him down," he ordered his confederates. "We got this old badger now—"

Shots rattled from all around him, and Ez was conscious of a chill running along his spine. He seemed fatally trapped. It was like Idaho Towner to wait for a sure thing and then strike without mercy.

An instant or two later a rifle rang out—*spang, spang*—followed by aroused yells. There was a tremendous crashing in a nearby thicket, and an enraged grizzly tumbled out, scrambling madly for the safety of the crags and aiming savage blows at anything in its way. Ez barely yanked his trembling pony out of its path.

One of Towner's men let out a yell of terror as the bear rushed by and disappeared into the brush. Just then, Pat Stevens, Sam and several others came plunging into view. They closed in around Idaho as if by accident, and Pat called out to Ez.

"What goes on here, Ez? Did you have that grizzly by the ears—or was it the other way around?"

Ez caught the double meaning in Pat's query. "Close brush," he tossed back coolly. "But I reckon that bear served Towner's purpose well enough!"

10.

"WHAT'S the answer here, Towner?" Pat challenged Idaho, although perfectly aware of what the outlaw had been about. "Throwing lead kind of carelessly, weren't you?"

"Could be." Idaho grinned brazenly. "A man's apt to get a little excited with a grizzly underfoot. I did my best to nail him."

"Quite sure it was the bear you were trying to get, are you?"

Towner gave him an insolent look. "What are you trying to prove, Stevens?"

Pat turned to Ez. "Anything more to say, Ezra?" The tall tracker saw that Pat was ready to push the proof of Idaho's treachery to the limit.

"No harm done, boy," Ez drawled, his manner elaborately casual. "I might've got in the way of a slug or two. Could be my own fault." He gave Towner a polite nod. "After this I'll watch the—bears closer."

Idaho's confederates turned away, their stony faces hiding their disappointment. The incident seemed ended. "Hope we didn't lose all those mustangs in the hassle," a man growled.

Moving into the open, they rode down to the rope-and-post fence that made an enclosed corral of the canyon's upper reaches. Hurled into a panic by the grizzly, some dozen or so of the threescore horses had knocked a wide hole in the barrier. Avery and the other guard, aided by several hunters, were hazing the strays back inside and some of the other men had started to repair the gap. At a rough estimate, only three or four head had escaped.

When the repairs were completed, Gabe Marsh waved the men back to their work on the trap. Riding in groups, the horse hunters talked the affair over. Pat failed to overhear any comments indicating that these men understood Idaho Towner's true object. Idaho himself rode boldly among them, trading on his exploits with the grizzly.

Failure had only made Idaho bolder, his escape from swift retribution swelling his self-confidence. Ez accepted his brazen pretensions with surprising restraint, but did not slacken in his determination that the renegade should perform his full share of the work on the wing trap. Idaho seethed under this treatment, but a further clash was avoided during the remainder of the afternoon, and Marsh professed himself well satisfied with progress as they jogged back to camp.

Pat and his friends were still bedding down in an isolated corner of the camp. Most of the horse hunters preferred to separate and spread out for the night. During the meal and afterward Towner clowned boisterously about the fires, ingratiating himself with the men.

"We posting a watch tonight?" Sam muttered as they rolled up in their blankets.

"Idaho's smarter than that," Pat pointed out. "We'll give him the chance to outsmart himself."

Ez was strongly in favor of overpowering Towner some dark night and delivering him to the marshal. But Stevens felt sure Marsh would never allow them to get away with this. "He must have a pretty shrewd idea of what Towner is," Pat explained, "but he's using us all for his work, and the work comes first. That won't stop me for a minute," he added soberly. "We'll just have to watch our chance—unless Idaho makes it for us."

On the following day Idaho abruptly altered his tactics. While the horse hunters were wolfing their breakfast, he advanced without warning on Cash Avery. "What's this I hear you're saying about me, Avery?" he demanded menacingly.

Avery was an inoffensive soul, doing his work without complaint and saying little to anyone. But he had nerve. He coolly finished his coffee before he spoke. "What did you hear?"

"You said I was a damned nuisance yesterday when that grizzly got in the horse corral!" Towner charged harshly.

Avery shrugged, turning his back on Idaho, who was three or four inches taller and sixty pounds heavier than he was.

Idaho savagely whirled him around. "*You* said it," he bullied Avery. "Now you'll back it up—" He broke off short, feeling a hard object thrust into his back.

"Little mistake on your part, Towner," a voice murmured behind him. "*I* said it, if you got to know!"

Livid, Idaho turned cautiously to meet Ezra's bleak stare. The big fellow displayed surprising presence of mind. "Never mind the cover-up," he rasped. "Take your gun out of my ribs, Ezra."

"I'll plant a slug there if you ask for it once more," Ez grated.

It was useless for Towner to look to his confederates for aid before the watchful men. Breathing hard, he glared his implacable defiance. But Ez had already been fully warned where this man was concerned. Not in the least intimidated, he stepped back, sheathing his gun.

"We figuring to do some work today or not?" he tossed at Gabe Marsh carelessly.

Gabe was staring at them both with sour disfavor. "I'm warning you two right now—I won't have any more of this trouble-making. You stop it, or I'll stop it. Do you hear?"

"I reckon," Ez assented with a hard grin. Idaho said nothing.

They started at once for the wing trap, where they put in a hard morning. Towner made a further nuisance of himself with sarcastic remarks and was obviously spoiling for more trouble. At the noon break when all knocked off to rest and eat, Stevens saw it coming when Idaho, who was moving about restlessly seeking shade, finally halted before Avery, now comfortably ensconced under a protecting rock.

"Crawl out of there, you," he ordered roughly.

Without moving, Avery peered up at him. "What now—?"

Idaho leaned forward, hands on hips. "I said get out!" he roared.

After a pause Cash sat up and finally rose to his feet. He stood there while the burly outlaw calmly usurped his comfortable resting place. Pat and Sam watched Avery move away without protest.

"Side-stepping trouble," the stout man muttered softly. He had seen Avery's cold, emotionless face. "But I don't think Cash is as worried as Towner thinks he is—"

Pat made no comment. He saw the inevitable clash coming. Probably Avery recognized it too. Cash averted trouble during the afternoon by keeping out of Idaho's way.

They labored late, striving to complete the trap. Ez made a last-minute survey with Marsh and pronounced the wings completed satisfactorily. "Tomorrow we'll finish masking them, and you can get that corral pushed along, too," the big tracker planned. "Then we'll be in business."

Interest in the coming test of the new trap held the horse hunters in talk as they moved back to camp at dusk. Several busied themselves with the cook fires, and for a time all was bustle and rough sport as supper went forward. An air of good-humored anticipation animated them all.

The meal ready, they fell to with voracious appetite. Darkness had fallen; the glow of the fires illuminated the dark moving figures, filling the canyon with wavering shadows.

Pat and the partners were keeping a constant watch on Idaho Towner, who was seated cross-legged at the next fire while he ate. Trouble started when Cash Avery came over to their own fire to strike up a casual acquaintance with Ezra. Striding past the spot where Towner was seated, Avery did not so much as take notice of the outlaw; but, glancing up, Idaho looked after him calculatingly for a moment and then jumped to his feet.

Avery was making a remark to Ez, when Towner came barging forward. He swung Cash around with a jerk that all but dislocated the smaller man's arm. "What's the big idea now?" roared Idaho.

Forcing his arm free, Avery looked at Idaho with undisguised hatred. "You again? What's eating you to-night, Towner?"

"You kicked over my coffee!"

Pat happened to know that nothing of the kind had happened. He had seen Towner deliberately knock over the tin container himself. Nevertheless, he grabbed Sam's arm, quickly silencing his protest. "Watch this," he muttered under his breath.

Avery's jaw squared. "Didn't," he rasped flatly.

"I say you did!" Towner raised his harsh voice in a bellow. "I'll break your neck! I've had a bellyful of you as it is—!"

The brutal taunt triggered Cash Avery's stolid temper. He plunged squarely at Towner, his fist slashing up. The blow caught Idaho alongside the jaw and he stumbled back, recovering his balance with a roar. Avery followed him up closely. Sixty pounds lighter, he knew he had to work fast. He struck again at Towner. Idaho threatened to stumble backward. Catching himself, he swept his heavy arm around like a scythe. Lifted and flung sidewise, Avery landed sprawling on hands and knees squarely in the fire.

Cash rolled away instantly, but not before the flames had licked a part of his beard away. He slapped madly at the sparks, lurching to his feet. In contrast to Towner's savage cursing, Avery was deathly silent now. His hand streaked to his holster. If he could have grasped his gun then, Idaho would have perished on the spot. But Cash's Colt had bounced out when he had fallen.

With a snarl Idaho charged at him. Avery tried to dodge, but the big outlaw's driving knee caught him on the point of the shoulder and tumbled him afresh. Towner pounced on him, roaring like some berserk savage. He lifted Cash up bodily and slammed him to the ground with a bone-shaking thump.

Avery had stamina. He struggled to his knees and dived at Idaho's legs. Getting a grip somehow, he heaved upward. Towner's balance wavered. Then he came down like a crashing tree across Cash's back, flattening the smaller man, and both sprawled in the dust.

This time it was plain the struggle was telling heavily on Avery. Dazed, his breath tearing stertorously from his lungs, he was unable to prevent Idaho from violently tumbling him over. Towner grasped his adversary's arm, and thrusting out a stout knee, he stretched the arm across it, deliberately and ruthlessly bringing his weight to bear down on it till the bones snapped with an audible, sickening crunch.

It was done so quickly that the incredulous watchers had no time to intervene before it was over.

"Here, you—!"

The cry tore from Ezra's lips as he sprang forward. Grasping Idaho by the shirt collar, he hurled the treacherous renegade backward.

Towner vented a bawl like that of an infuriated bull. Tumbled headlong, he came swiftly to his knees; but Ez never let him get set. Jamming a heel against Idaho's shoulder, he rammed him backward. Again crashing down, the outlaw had barely struggled up on all fours when Ezra's sweeping blow caught him flush in the neck and flung him half-a-dozen feet.

Dazed and gasping, Towner was in bad shape. Ez stalked forward and, hauling Idaho up by his shirtfront, planted a solid six-inch jab into his blood-smeared face. Idaho hit the ground with a sodden thud. He sought weakly to struggle up, only to fall back.

"How do you like it?" Ez yelled at him stridently. "I ought to crack your dirty neck!"

Hands on their guns, Idaho's cronies attempted to crowd forward, seeking a clear aim at Ezra. Sam Sloan blocked them, and the guns of half-a-dozen angry horse hunters were menacingly displayed.

"Keep out of this, Lackey—you too, Barnes!" a man warned tightly. "Towner only got what he's handing out!"

"Stand aside," snapped Lackey, striving to overawe Sam. "We'll settle this here and now. Your long-shanked pard didn't have no call to jump Idaho from behind!"

Glowering, Sam measured the pair. "So maybe you want me to tackle you both—from the front."

"Here, here. That'll be plenty now." Gabe Marsh made up his mind it was time to interfere. "Drop it where you are, savvy?" There was an authoritative sound in his voice that halted further hostilities.

Every man in camp meanwhile had crowded about, intently following developments. They pointedly avoided Towner's proximity, giving him plenty of room. The big outlaw possessed considerable recuperative powers; in the rumble of muttered talk which followed Gabe's ultimatums, he drew himself to his feet.

"Ezra!" he bawled, leveling a blunt forefinger at Ez. "Mighty big with your fists, you are, when a man's back is turned. I'm not overlooking this!"

A hush fell in which Ezra, standing a dozen feet away, regarded Idaho narrowly. "What will you do?" he countered scathingly.

"Why don't you grab for that gun of yours," Idaho challenged thickly. "Or is that a part of your nervy bluff?"

Ez deliberately turned his back. "I won't even blow your brains out just to suit you," he retorted with a humorless laugh.

Idaho looked fit to be tied, his corded features scarlet. "I'll tear your head off your shoulders yet, you one-eyed monkey!"

Ez made no reply whatever. Paying solicitous heed to the setting of Avery's broken forearm, he seemed to have forgotten Towner's existence.

"Towner!" Gabe Marsh threw the force of his will against the outlaw. "By Godfrey, this settles it. You asked to join my crowd. But you don't work. You don't give a hoot if we catch mustangs or not! So far," he stated flatly, "you've done nothing but make trouble, pick fights and hinder us to suit yourself. That'll stop right here and now, because I'll see that it does."

Idaho glanced at him with hard self-possession. "What would that mean?" he growled.

"It means you're washed up," was the uncompromising response. "You're not only useless, but you put out of commission a man worth twice what you are. . . . You can pull up stakes and drift—you and your pals!"

"No, you don't." Idaho raised his harsh voice. "Trying to clip me of my share of the horses we already snagged, are you? I'll have your liver, Marsh, before you get away with that!"

Pat was following this attentively, unwilling to see the renegade driven beyond his surveillance. Gabe himself appeared perplexed by the justice of Towner's argument. He shook his head dourly. "We don't owe you a thing."

"You'll find that you do," Idaho answered smoothly. "This is a tip, Marsh! Try to drive me out of here, and you'll never collect a dollar from those horses."

Gabe's mouth worked. He hated to be threatened, but he must have guessed the promise would be ruthlessly carried out. Somehow he kept his temper.

"All right, Idaho." His tone was flat. "You want your pay, and we'll let you earn it. Just see that you do Avery's work as well as your own, and we're even. But remember—" the warning crackled sharply—"one more of these show-off plays of yours, and I'll make it my affair to settle with you personally. That's sure as death, and you'll find it surer!"

Nevertheless, Idaho Towner was fully aware of having scored a victory. Just as clearly, he counted on the common knowledge of his naked brutality to insure him a certain freedom of action.

11.

NERVES were strung taut in the horse hunters' camp the following day.

There were few but expected a further clash between Towner and Ezra. Gabe Marsh put this off for a few hours at least by sending Ez with a handful of men to finish masking the trap wings.

A mustang band of uncommon size had been reported some half-dozen miles to the west. Leaving a couple of hands to guard the camp and look after Cash Avery, the rest of the party set out in high spirits to investigate this.

Stevens went along with them. He was nonplussed as the morning wore on to note that Towner didn't make the slightest effort to escape from constant surveillance. He knew better, however, than to relax his vigilance.

The men sighted the wild horse herd far off across a broad basin. They spent an hour trying to draw close enough to examine the animals in detail, but the band broke up and scattered over a wide area. Marsh promptly called off the chase.

"Let's not drive 'em out of the country," he ruled. "That's a plenty big enough bunch to try out our trap on. We'll give them a day to cool off and drift together."

They turned back across the long sage slopes, animosities forgotten for the moment in animated discussion of the rich possibilities. Some claimed to have spotted valuable horses, and there was little doubt that a successful catch would net a substantial profit.

Reaching camp an hour after midday, the men were still busily talking as they prepared a belated meal. Pat was making sure Idaho did not quietly remount and ride off to catch Ezra unawares at the wing trap when a shout arose from across the camp.

"Somebody coming!" a man sang out. "It's a wagon, Marsh. Must be them supplies you arranged for—"

All looked that way. But not even Pat guessed what was coming until the high-piled buckboard came rolling in through the gap in the pines drawn by a spirited team of bays, and the identity of the pair on the spring seat was revealed. Bobby Durgen held the lines, and Kit Majors was seated beside her, a rifle propped upright between his knees.

The horse hunters found nothing unusual in their arrival. Several called out in greeting. Camp supplies had been running low the past few days, and the men would be pleased to see them replenished.

But Stevens frowned at the appearance of the girl. Finding himself not far from Gabe Marsh at the moment, he stepped quickly toward him. "What does this mean, Marsh?" He waved toward the wagon.

Gabe's glance was casual. "It means I arranged with Ducks Durgen to send out fresh supplies by a certain date," he told Pat. "We need them—and he was glad to get the business. Anything wrong with that?"

Pat dropped it there. Clearly Durgen had had no one else but his daughter to send. She was here now. Knowing her stout spirit, Stevens was only surprised that Bobby had consented to let Majors accompany her at all.

As Kit handed the girl down and the men took charge of the team, Pat looked about sharply to see whether Idaho had noted this arrival. The renegade was not in evidence at the moment; but even as Pat allowed himself to entertain the slim hope that the supplies could be unloaded and the young couple take their departure unnoted, several men came stamping through the nearby fringe of underbrush, and Towner himself stepped into the open.

Idaho stopped abruptly. Pat did not miss the wicked

flare in Idaho's cold eyes as he saw what he believed were the two sole witnesses to the murder of Lyte Majors.

Bobby and Kit were instantly aware of his presence. The puncher froze. He opened his lips, starting to speak impulsively. But the girl quickly put a hand on his arm, murmuring a word or two which only Majors caught. He clamped a rigid control on himself.

Towner himself appeared on the verge of barging forward. But Sam coolly intervened, stepping in front of him. "Your turn to ride herd on the horse corral tonight, ain't it, mister?" he demanded colorlessly.

Idaho read the covert warning in this direction. He stood irresolute, deflected from his headlong purpose.

Bobby Durgen read the tension in this moment. Her face wore a strained expression. "If you'll have your men unload the supplies, Mr. Marsh, we'll get started back at once," she said. "Father will be looking for us."

Gabe heard her out with an indulgent smile. "Take it easy, girl. Rest a while," he advised kindly. "We're right glad to have that stuff, and it was good of Durgen to send it along a day or so ahead. But you'll be going back light. Sit down there by the fire, you two, and Tennessee will make a pot of coffee."

Bobby shook her head. "Father is alone at the store, and he can't get about. We must go back as soon as possible." But she did not insist further, remaining near Majors and glancing about the canyon uneasily.

Kit was all for action of some kind. "Why shouldn't we tell Marsh?" Pat overheard his fierce mutter to the girl. But she shook her head again decisively.

Stevens understood her decision to remain silent. To reveal Idaho Towner's true identity to these men could serve as no surprise and would only make the situation more awkward for Majors and herself, since it would force Idaho's enmity into the open. The girl knew well enough that Gabe Marsh did not regard himself as a law officer. He would undertake nothing that would interfere with the work of trapping mustangs. If Towner's savage treachery

was unleashed now, she and Kit would be forced to cope
with it as best they could, unaided.

With some dim comprehension of this, Majors was
anxious enough to get away without delay. "Where do
you want these supplies, Marsh?" He spoke roughly, the
urgency plain in his tone.

Gabe shrugged. "We'll get the wagon unloaded for
you." He pointed out a shaded spot under the pines where
the supplies might be piled. "Lead the team over here,
Nueces," he instructed one of his men. "The rest of you
boys can pitch in and help."

Kit hurried that way. Idaho followed the other men, a
lethal gleam in his eye. Doubtless, he was waiting to get
close enough to the young fellow to turn on him. Throwing Sam a warning look, Stevens made haste to accompany them.

While the wagon was being unloaded, Pat and Sam
managed to keep Idaho separated from the object of his
hatred. More than once, one or the other deliberately
stepped in between just as Towner attempted to crowd in
next to the doggedly working puncher. The big outlaw
gave them stares of baffled fury.

But Idaho did not intend to allow this unforeseen opportunity to slip by without some effort to grasp it. "Blowflies
been at this beef," he growled as another man shouldered
a side. "Why didn't you bother to cover it, kid?" He shot
Kit a contemptuous glare.

The young fellow's mouth flew open, ready with a
stinging retort, then clamped shut.

Idaho waited only for a moment before he tried it again.
"Where in hell's the airtights?" he rapped disparagingly.
"Ain't that dump of Durgen's got anything but beans?"

That was too much for Kit's overstrung nerves. Before
anyone could prevent it, he hurled himself on the burly
outlaw, fists swinging. A smashing blow caught Towner
on his bruised mouth, and another crashed into his ribs.

The unexpectedness of the assault threw him back, but
only momentarily. With a roar Idaho caught himself, and,
with a swing of his arm, flung Kit sprawling. Kit was up

in a flash. Again he charged, driving straight toward Towner's midriff.

The breath went out of Idaho with a *whoosh*. He clubbed Majors across the shoulders with his massive fist, and again the lighter man went down. This time he strove to grab the outlaw's legs and upset him. Idaho kicked savagely, then reached down and grabbed Kit, hauling him aloft by sheer brute strength. Down he slammed the puncher with shattering impact, flat in the dirt. Next instant Idaho started to leap forward, clearly intending to jump on the young fellow's back with grinding boots. But the horse hunters were watching this conflict closely. They had no intention of letting Towner cripple another man as he had Cash Avery. A dozen hard hands grabbed Idaho, hauling him roughly back in the nick of time.

"No, you don't, Idaho!" cried a man hoarsely. "We've seen enough of your playful tricks!"

When Kit leaped up ready to spring to the attack once more, others thrust him aside, forcing him apart from Towner. "Leave it alone, boy," he was advised flatly. "You don't know this hombre. He was just egging you on for this!"

Majors struggled for a minute or two, recognized Sam Sloan, and relaxed. He saw Stevens among the men restraining Towner, but was quick enough to avoid making any sign of recognition.

"Maybe I don't know Idaho," he challenged defiantly. "But he'll know me next time. Turn him loose—I'll tackle that big loudmouth, any time or anywhere!"

But the horse hunters would not allow this. They forced Kit back, and Gabe Marsh came striding over. "What is this foolishness?" he bellowed sternly.

"The bantam here pitched into Idaho," a man explained, half inclined to grin. "We broke it up."

Gabe wheeled on Majors. "I'm willing to agree now you don't belong here, boy," he censured him. "Don't you know better than to tackle a man twice your heft?"

"Why don't *you* wake up, Marsh?" Kit snapped. "You

must be awful short of help. If you don't know it yet, that bird is a crook and a killer!''

Tension stretched taut as a bow-string in the following silence. Kit's fiery temper had caused him to spill the beans, and every man in the canyon waited on edge. Whatever his own lively suspicions were, however, Gabe only growled, ''Oh, now—get hold of yourself. It don't pay off to go calling names.''

''You'll never get shot for being too smart, that's sure,'' Kit retorted. ''If you need any telling, Marsh, it was Idaho Towner who stole my father's roan herd, and then he—''

The remainder of his indictment was drowned in Idaho's bellow of protest. ''What are you trying to feed us?'' Somehow the renegade summoned up a snarl of contemptuous mirth. ''Do you still wonder why I tried to slap that mouthy punk down, Marsh? . . . Let loose of me—'' he struggled with the men restraining him—''I don't have to put up with this kind of guff—!''

The horse hunters forced Idaho back, advising him to get hold of himself. It was plain they were prepared to discount young Kit's direct accusations on the score of passion. ''Slack it off, Idaho,'' one urged tartly. ''You threw the hooks into him, and naturally he came back at you. He'll be on his way soon, so what do you care?''

''I won't allow any such talk about me,'' roared Towner. ''By grab, if I can't square this with that runt now, I'll do it my own way!''

''No, you won't.'' Pat spoke up flatly. ''We saw how you argue things out with anyone you don't happen to like. You'll stay right here and tend to business—you insisted on that a day ago.''

Idaho glared at him implacably, and the outlaw's two associates pushed close to argue hotly with Stevens. Pat fended them off, well aware of their purpose. As long as they could keep the argument fixed on irrelevancies, attention would be diverted from Kit's damning charges against Towner.

Marsh abruptly took charge of the situation. ''Go on up there to the corral fence and stand your guard,'' he told

Idaho levelly. "I've had all of this crazy hassle I intend to put up with. You hear me, Idaho?"

Idaho flung himself free of the men holding him, but he neither did as he was told, nor showed any signs of intention to do so.

Gabe stared at him for a moment and turned away. "Get that wagon empty, and do it on the jump," he ordered gruffly.

As the others hastened to comply, Pat made sure that he saw all that went on. Towner stood muttering with his hard-faced cronies a good many yards away from the wagon where Kit doggedly pushed the work of unloading. It seemed unlikely that any further clash was imminent.

It did not escape Stevens when Marsh moved over to join Bobby Durgen near the fire. He strained to catch their low exchange of words.

"I don't savvy this." Gabe was regarding the girl with unconcealed perplexity. "You come in here to unload a few supplies—and it touches this uproar off. Idaho ain't easy to get along with, and that's a fact. But—" He broke off tentatively, waiting.

Bobby did not take the clumsily offered bait. "I said before that we ought to be on our way," she returned uneasily, glancing about. "Father is still waiting for me."

"Sure. You'll be off directly, if that's what you want." Marsh could not down his curiosity so readily, however. "But that young fighting cock is sure on the prod," he insisted. "A man would think he'd tangled with Towner before this—"

Pat hovered close, ready to intervene if Gabe's gruff solicitude showed any signs of breaking down the girl's taut reserve. It was not only Bobby's own safety with which Stevens was concerned. There was no telling what Towner's explosive response would be if specific and dangerous charges were flung in his face. Certainly it would more than likely imperil Pat's own purpose of taking the outlaw in charge when the time was ripe.

"Kit is worrying about me," she evaded quickly. "That— man criticized our supplies, although they are what you ordered, and Kit knows that Father depends on your good will.''

Gabe grunted. ''I don't listen to him. Towner's been away from camp off and on,'' he pursued. ''You sure he didn't turn up there at the store, ma'am?''

''Once or twice,'' Bobby said vaguely. ''I—know him by sight. . . . Isn't the wagon about unloaded now?''

There was no mistaking her urgent anxiety to be off. Gabe was about to reply reassuringly when Idaho raised his voice in a harsh call. ''What's all the private chatter over there, Marsh? Let us in on it.''

Gabe gazed across at him fixedly. ''Afraid I'll hear something about you, are you, Idaho?''

''You wouldn't listen to me five minutes ago,'' Towner fired back. ''Let's be fair about this—before I see to it myself.''

It seemed to Stevens that every added word would only make things worse for Bobby and Kit once they got away from the horse camp. Fortunately, Marsh paid the renegade no further attention, and turned to the men at the wagon. ''That the last piece, Eph? All right. swing the wagon around here.'' He looked at Bobby. ''I expect you've got our bill all toted up, h'mm?''

The girl drew a folded paper from the pocket of her skirt. She handed it over. ''We're not at all worried about this, Mr. Marsh. But Dad thought you might ask for it.''

Marsh studied the bill briefly, checking the items off. He nodded. ''I made sure we had enough money to cover our needs till we make a sale.'' He started to pull out a wallet.

''No, I—'' She halted him abruptly. ''I'd just as soon not carry the money with me, if you don't mind.''

''Well, I always pay my bills when they fall due. I like it that way.''

''Mr. Marsh. Please.'' Bobby was frankly pleading.

''Like that, eh?'' He looked at her quickly, stowing the wallet back out of sight. ''I savvy. We'll pay this bill the first time I'm anywhere near the store. . . . Now, you two—'' his gesture took in Kit, who was grimly waiting— ''climb aboard and clear out of here, both of you.''

12.

PAT knew the real danger for Kit Majors and Bobby would come when the buckboard pulled away from the doubtful safety of the horse camp. "Hold it right here, Marsh," he spoke up clearly. "I want to get this straight. You don't mean you're shoving these youngsters off to get home the best way they can—?" His tone was incredulous.

About to turn back to their own concerns, the horse hunters delayed to hear this. Gabe's look was blank.

"Why not?" he asked sharply. "They got here all right, didn't they? They ought to know the way home!"

If Gabe was deliberately misunderstanding, Pat did not leave him long in doubt. "That's got nothing to do with it," he retorted. "You saw what happened here. For some reason, Towner holds a grudge against this pair. I don't trust him for a minute. He'll wipe Majors out, given the smallest chance—"

Idaho himself was following this talk with strained attention. For reasons of his own he said nothing, waiting for Gabe's reply. Marsh was less reticent. "What nonsense!" he exclaimed. "I told Idaho where he stands, Stevens! He's here for work and he'll do it."

"I say he'll disappear twenty minutes after Majors and that girl pull out of the canyon," declared Pat flatly. "I know what he's up to, and I won't stand for it."

With no patience for anything that threatened to delay his work, Gabe chose to be stubborn. "Give me one reason why Idaho's so anxious to knock Majors off, since you're so sure of it."

Pat could have given him a conclusive answer. He was well aware of the fact that, once Towner knew that he and his friends had also witnessed Lyte Majors' murder, the outlaw would promptly lose all interest in Kit and Bobby. At the same time, Stevens knew that to reveal his own interest in Towner would be to put an end to any chance he and the partners might have of grabbing the outlaw.

"Towner gave his own reasons when he piled into a man half his size," he evaded. "I'm going on what I've already seen, Marsh—and you ought to have enough savvy to understand it. Put Idaho under close guard for half a day" he urged. "That will satisfy me. And you can sleep better!"

From his expression, Gabe had manifestly had enough of the rivalry between these men. He whirled toward Idaho, raising his voice. "What about it, Towner? You heard him! Anything to say?" he snapped tartly.

Idaho read what it meant. His murderous glower at Pat spoke volumes. But he kept his hands a safe distance away from his gun. "Just keep it up, Stevens," he contented himself with tossing back. "You're old enough to dig your own grave!"

Pat ignored this jab, bearing down on Marsh, without letup. "There you are, Gabe. If it isn't one of us Towner is threatening, it's another. If you don't do something about him, I'll see that you're held to account for whatever happens."

"Fine." Marsh's irony was grating. "I'll tell you what you can do. Since nothing else will suit you, Stevens, you and your friends can guard them kids on their way home— and I hope that suits you. It better," he added sternly, "because you'll be out of pay till you get back!"

"Oh no." Pat turned this proposal down decisively. "It was you who ordered those supplies sent out here—and you who were so anxious for help that you took Towner on. Don't shove your responsibility off on me."

Gabe's resentful stare betrayed his exasperation. "You're taking a mighty strange interest in other folks, mister.

Suppose I fire you and your pards here and now and send you on your way. What then?'' he barked.

"You can do that." Pat's reply was level. "And if Majors and this girl wind up in some canyon with a smashed wagon on top of them, it's still your headache, Marsh. For you've been warned.''

He did not have to raise his voice to make his point. Gabe was now driven into a corner. "All right!" he bawled. "You're so smart, we'll see if you can take orders! You birds can watch Towner yourselves. And I'll expect the same amount of work of you all as I did before.''

"We'll just do that." Pat's calm came as a surprise. He waved Kit and Bobby on their way. "You'll get through okay," he told them. "Don't give it another thought.''

With tightly pressed lips, the puncher grasped the reins and started to turn the rig. He was far from happy, but he had to be satisfied. "Don't ask Durgen to make any more deliveries to your tough camp," he called to Marsh as the vehicle started away. "If a man rides in to pick up a pack or two, send somebody besides Idaho Towner—or he won't get a thing!''

The buckboard passed beyond the curtain of pines, gathering speed on its way toward the canyon's mouth and the open range. The afternoon was waning. Pat knew Majors was anxious to make as much distance as possible before darkness forced the wagon down to a crawling pace, if it did not halt progress altogether.

The sound of the grating wheels had barely died away when Ezra put in an appearance, riding back to camp with the men who had been helping to complete the wing trap on the slope. Marsh was waiting for them. "All done over there, Ezra?" he called gruffly.

"All done, Gabe. Horse-high and hog-tight," Ez announced with satisfaction. "All we need now is mustangs.''

The leader held him in talk for some minutes while the other men set about making ready for supper. The one-eyed tracker glanced casually about, but it was not long before he shrewdly gathered that something was afoot. He noted that Towner and his pals were keeping to them-

selves, and it did not escape his notice that Stevens and
Sam Sloan were pointedly watching the trio.

"What now, boy?" Ez muttered, the minute he was
able to snatch a private word with Pat. "Another run-in
with that ornery gazebo?"

Pat quickly told him what had happened following the
arrival of Majors and Ducks Durgen's daughter. "Towner
would murder them in a second," he concluded. "And
this would have been his chance to catch them together if I
hadn't blocked the deal."

Ez glanced across at Idaho. "How sure are you that we
can keep him here long enough for them to get clear
away?" he asked.

Pat shrugged. "We can try—but there's no point in
taking chances." He turned as Sam came up, lowering his
voice to a murmur. "Sam, sometime in the next twenty
minutes I want you to drift away without attracting attention to yourself. Ez and I will camp on Towner's tail. Push
off after Kit and the girl," he directed, "but don't join
them. Hang back a quarter-mile or so and keep a careful
watch all around you. If Towner *should* give us the slip,
he'll still have you to get past. Have you got it?"

Sam's eagerness to be off could be detected in his
extremely casual manner. He had his own way of going
about it, strolling pointedly past Idaho and his confederates
and treating them to a studied stare. If they repaid this
attention with interest, it got them nowhere, and they
presently fell to ignoring his movements altogether.

The next time the renegades glanced up from their fire,
peering about warily, Sloan seemed to have disappeared.
But Towner saw that Stevens was regarding them alertly
and that Ez was not far away, ready for anything.

Ez and Pat conferred a few minutes later. "I think he
caught on already," the tall tracker muttered, jerking his
chin in the direction of the outlaw.

Pat's grunt was one of indifference. "I got that. It
doesn't seem to bother him either." He turned this over
soberly. "It says to me that they're cooking up something
that they're even more interested in."

Ez nodded. "They may even figure Sam's in the pines trying to listen to 'em. . . . We better stand watch tonight." He had provided himself with a rifle, and it was to be observed that he kept its barrel tilted constantly in the general direction of the renegades.

Done eating, the horse hunters had their smoke about the campfires. Gabe Marsh kept his eye on Pat and Ezra, making no comment. As the fires died down, the men turned to their bedrolls, and quiet descended on the camp.

It was Ez who provoked a brief outburst twenty minutes later by boldly tossing additional fuel on the fire around which the three renegades lay, thus illuminating their blanketed forms. Idaho rose up abruptly. "Get away from that fire, you!" he ordered violently.

Ez coolly tossed another stick on the blaze. Instead of answering, he turned back toward Pat at the other fire. "Shall I knock him on the head?" he called out.

Idaho made a feint at leaping out of his blankets, but he did not follow it through. Ez deliberately waited for him, a challenge in his very lack of excitement. Snarling, Towner sank back, rolling his face away from the light, and silence returned to the canyon.

Making ready to turn in for a few hours' rest while Ez stood guard, Stevens watched this byplay carefully. When the lanky man came back a moment later, Pat commented, "That was a smart move, Ez. Keep that fire going, no matter what he says, and we've got that slippery hombre licked this time."

Ezra smiled grimly. "I'll keep it going."

Half an hour later he was back to replenish Towner's dying fire. Idaho exploded afresh. "Blast you, Ezra! I don't intend to stay awake all night with a light in my eyes to please you!"

"What'll you do about it, neighbor?" Ez asked coolly.

Idaho acted in a flash. Cursing savagely, he whipped out the gun he must have had concealed under his blanket. Ez leaped aside at the first glint of steel, grabbing for his own weapon. But for once it was not at him that the outlaw fired. At the first crashing explosion, the blazing fire burst apart with a shower of sparks as if a bomb had struck it. Another crack, and it was virtually blown into extinction.

Ez vented a wrathful exclamation. His own Colt slammed, the slug tearing into the blanket roll where Towner had lain a bare second ago. Ez sprang to kick the fire together, building it into a blaze with a handful of dry pine needles.

Jerked awake by the first shot, Pat came rushing over. "Never mind the fire," he cried. "Grab that wolf before he makes his break!"

They were too late, however. In the pause that followed, the thud of running boots came to their ears. Towner had carefully planned his escape, and it was clear that the attempt might well be successful. But Pat and Ezra had kept saddled ponies near at hand for just such an emergency. As the fire blazed up once more, the dry twigs catching, Pat turned on Towner's confederates, sitting up in their beds uncertain of what it was all about, if their manner could be trusted.

"Grab your bronc and tear for the mouth of the canyon, Ez," he ordered sharply. "I'll ride herd on these daisies— and with any luck Idaho can't get past you!"

Despite the chorus of harsh, indignant complaints from the awakening horse hunters, the one-eyed man swung astride and raced clattering down the canyon. Pat calmly threw plenty of wood on the fire and squatted on his heels to watch.

"I won't put up with much more of this, Stevens," Gabe Marsh burst out from his distant bed.

Pat did not bother to reply.

An hour passed. The late moon rose, sailing above the canyon wall. It cast sharp black and white shadows about the camp, shedding its light on the figures of Idaho Towner's pals. Only then did Stevens allow the fire to die down. Shortly afterward Ezra came cantering back to camp alone.

"No luck, eh?"

Ez appeared moody. "He didn't pass me. With that

moon, he might've climbed out over the canyonside. It could be done. . . ."

Pat took it quietly. "We gave Majors and Bobby a good start," he summed up. "The rest is up to Sam. Grab some shut-eye, Ez, and you can spell me later."

"Shucks." Ezra cast a dark glance toward the motionless renegades. "Why not stake that pair out and get our rest?"

Pat waved him away.

Later the tall redhead relieved him. The sullen pair they watched were still in evidence the following morning.

As soon as the camp began to stir, Gabe Marsh strode over to Pat and Ez. "Well," he said gruffly, taking a deliberate look around, "Idaho did give you the slip, after all, eh?"

Pat favored him with a curt nod. "You were warned what would happen, Gabe."

Marsh shunted away from this fast. "Ain't you going after him?"

"No." Pat would vouchsafe no more.

Gabe moved away, but he did not leave the matter alone. After breakfast he drifted back to accost Towner's companions. "Where would you say Idaho is off to, Lackey?" he asked one, pretending no more than ordinary interest.

Lackey glanced at him briefly. "Don't know." Whether or not he was aware of Ezra's unwavering scrutiny, he clearly had no interest in imparting so much as a guess. Marsh turned to the other.

"What about it, Barnes? Did Towner tell you anything?" he pressed.

"It could be he got tired of this place, Gabe," Barnes offered ingenuously. "Idaho goes by streaks—and ever since Stevens and these other birds drifted in here, we been stalling, building a silly fence and like that. No chasing horses at all, and Idaho gets bored." He had more to say, but it summed up to the same thing.

The men stayed in camp that day, planning the details of the drive. As the discussions went on, again and again

Marsh glanced frowningly toward Stevens. He could not comprehend Pat's stolid indifference to Idaho's departure after all that had been said. Nor was he enlightened when, an hour after noon, Idaho Towner himself came jogging into the canyon, a glum look on his face. The horse hunters stared at him but prudently put no questions. Gabe was bolder.

"Where you been off to, Towner?" he questioned him bluntly.

Idaho looked around slowly, wholly ignoring Stevens and Ezra. "Nowhere," he growled, closing the subject with one word. Since he was covered with dust and his weary horse was a sad case, his answer was plainly a stall. Gabe made several tries with no better result before he gave up.

Pat and Ezra exchanged glances, a grim look of satisfaction touching the tall tracker's gaunt face. Neither he nor Stevens made a move until sunset. Then, after supper, Ez mounted his bronc and jogged quietly out of the canyon.

Marsh looked fretful at this. "Hanged if I know half of what's going on here," he complained.

An hour later Ez loomed up abruptly in the light of the fires with Sam Sloan at his side. The pair dismounted a little apart, and Ez made an imperative gesture. "Come over here, Stevens."

Pat joined them under the curious eyes of the camp. "Keep your voice down now," he warned. "Tell us what happened, Sam."

"Do you really need to ask?" the tubby little man drawled scornfully. "Idaho caught up with us just as you predicted, Stevens. He made a try for the wagon—and just never even got close."

"You tangled with him, eh?" growled Ez.

Sam's grin flashed out. "In a manner of speaking. I drove him off with my rifle, and he gave it up. I stayed with those kids for a couple of hours after Idaho disappeared, just to be sure. . . . Does that cover the case?"

Gabe came forward at that moment, ignoring their private conference. "Where did you go, Sloan, and what happened out there?" he demanded bluntly.

"Nary a thing, Marsh," Sam said. "All quiet and serene."

13.

"Boys we'll make a try at snapping that trap today, and see how it works," said Gabe Marsh next morning. The men were pleased. A rugged and capable lot, comparative inactivity coupled with the tension gripping the camp had made them restless. Even Cash Avery expressed interest, and the rest were eager for action.

Constant work on the wing trap for several days had given the mustangs a breather. The large herd discovered over west a few days before was still around, and smaller bands were drifting back into the region. Finishing his breakfast, tin coffee cup in hand, Marsh outlined his plan.

Gabe split his force into two groups. Using a stick, he indicated by marks in the dirt the area each was expected to cover. "The idea is to pick up a bunch of, say, twenty or thirty broomtails and head them south into the canyon," Marsh explained. "Once they're headed the right way, ram them hard. That way we won't be losing a lot of strays. Got it?"

"Then what Gabe?" a man put in.

"I'll want Ezra with me—and maybe one other man— out there below the trap. We'll do the rest," Marsh said. "We'll show ourselves at the right time and turn the mustangs up the slope. We'll soon find out if they'll head naturally for that low saddle, and we've got to crowd 'em close so they'll be inside those wings before they know it. A shot or two will stampede the stuff down into the corral—the gate shuts—and we've got them!"

It sounded simple enough and sure-fire. The horse hunters saddled up their mounts, commenting animatedly. Even Avery was coming along. "What are you up to, Cash?" a friend called. "You can't bucket around over the rocks with that busted arm."

"Won't try to," Avery gave back, gritting his teeth against the pain. "Gabe's posted me at the end of a rope near that trap corral. When you fog the broomies into it, I'll give a haul and slam the gate shut on 'em."

It made sense. Since Avery was eager to get into the action despite his useless arm, Marsh had shrewdly seen to it that his employment would release another man for the drive.

Pat had quietly managed to get himself and Sam included in the same group with Idaho Towner and his friends.

"You'll have to watch Towner's every move," Pat warned Sloan shortly. "After the check you handed him, he'll be itching to endorse it—and he might try it with a slug."

Sam's nod did not lack confidence. "Be an even better idea to stay right behind that baby," he growled. "He won't telegraph the news when he's ready to cut and run."

Pat was not seriously concerned on that score. "Towner must have learned by now that Ed Roman is in the country. You saw how fast he got back here after he missed his try at Kit and Bobby. Working with Marsh, at least he knows just who he's got to watch. Once away from the Uncompahgre, he can't be sure he can trust anybody."

Gabe was calling out from his saddle some distance off, urging them all on their way. "Get on with it, boys," he ordered brusquely. "We'll soon know whether we're in line to make a dollar or not."

They jogged out of the canyon into clear, fresh morning light. The tremendous sweep of the Uncompahgre lay outspread under the brilliant sunlight. All except Cash Avery avoided the wing trap today. Riding a couple of miles, they paused briefly at the point where Marsh, Ezra and a third man were to turn down into the canyon. Gabe issued final brisk instructions, and the horse hunters thrust on, splitting a short time afterwards into two groups which headed in different directions through the broken hills.

Combing a large reach of country between them and working gradually together, the two groups hoped to sweep up at least one unwary band of mustangs and turn it into the canyon toward the wing trap. Pat and Sam swung off toward the west with their group of seven or eight men. Towner and his two cronies were not calling attention to themselves today, jogging along quietly and taking instructions from the leader without protest. But the occasional icy glance which Idaho shot toward Sam revealed the nature of his smoldering thoughts. Intent on their purpose, the other horse hunters paid no heed to this byplay.

Within an hour several wild bands were sighted at a distance; but these were too small to rate particular attention. It was Sam who, twenty minutes later, pointed down through a shallow canyon indicating some two score horses grazing along a sage-studded slope. Willow and cottonwood protected their position somewhat, and this screen seemed likely to afford a means of convenient approach.

The leadership of this group had fallen to Lilholt, a Texan of enormous size. Coming lately from the Indian Territory, Lilholt was an old hand at outwitting the broomtails. Studying the situation briefly, he made his decision. "We'll loop right out around that bunch, spread out and flush them this way, boys," he said briefly. "Let's make it fast now. Gabe is waiting—"

Sticking to cover, they circled to windward of the unsuspecting band. Then, scattering out to cover a wide area, the riders closed in. Not till they showed themselves at a dozen points did the wild horses take alarm. There was a snort or two, heads tossing, a swift whistled warning—and then, wild as hawks, the mustangs swooped away with a rush, manes and tails whipping the wind.

Hanging back far enough to avoid alarming them unduly, the men pushed steadily on. Ten minutes later this caution bade fair to be their undoing. Driving his band ahead through a winding defile, the wily leader of the mustangs abruptly crowded his charges aside, slashing and nipping at their flanks in a desperate attempt to alter the direction of their flight.

Lilholt saw what was happening. "Close up!" he bellowed, waving the men that way. "Head 'em off there!"

Noting how Idaho hurled himself into this game with apparent enthusiasm, Pat and Sam swung the same way with the others. Up the slope and across the broken rocks they dashed, crowding the ponies to the utmost effort. For a few minutes it looked as if they would lose this race, but Lilholt urged them on with harsh yells. So well did Sloan respond despite his unwieldy bulk that he found himself forging to the front.

The racing mustangs were not yet ready to give up and turn back in the direction of the canyon and Lilholt swore in exasperation. "Swing 'em!" he roared. "Fire your guns—make a racket!"

Colts immediately cracked. To Sam's amazement and chagrin, his bronc suddenly broke stride. Before the stout man could prepare for what was coming, the roan abruptly crumpled and fell headlong, throwing its rider over its head. Sam rolled over twice and slammed up against a sturdy sage clump, breaking his fall.

Stevens swiftly reined that way, hauling up as Sam clambered to his feet. "What happened?" he called sharply.

Sam's bristly face hardened. "Can't you guess?" He strode back to his horse lying sprawled on the rocks and quickly confirmed his darkest suspicion. "The poor brute got taken with a sudden dose of lead poison, boy."

"That firing to turn the herd!" Pat exclaimed. "Towner grabbed his chance at you, eh—?"

Sam's nod expressed grim conviction. "It was probably meant for me. Idaho will deny it, of course. *He* won't know a thing about it! But are we letting this go along any further, Stevens?" he demanded.

Pat knew beyond doubt that the time had come to act. "No," he said deliberately. "Whatever he may guess about our object here, Idaho has got us marked for the same brand he puts on all his victims."

Sam was ready for immediate action. "Why not clamp down on that murdering rat here and now?"

Pat glanced about, considering. The horse hunters had raced on out of sight in pursuit of the mustangs; the pair were utterly alone here. "Not so fast," he cautioned Sam. "You're in no shape to move in on Idaho just now. But Nueces can't be far behind with those extra horses. . . . Climb up behind me, Sam. We'll pick up a bronc and join the others as fast as we can—then watch our chance. I'd suggest," he went on matter-of-factly, "waiting until those mustangs are headed well into the trap, if we can get there in time. Everybody will be excited and busy. We'll close in on Towner and take him cold before he suspects a thing. If those cronies of his stick their noses into it, we'll blast them fast."

"What if Marsh should happen to see that?" Sam asked, eyes glinting.

"If he does," said Pat, "we'll simply crowd the deal through. I'm not letting anything block me this time. . . . Climb up, will you?"

Ten minutes later they found Nueces trailing after the drive with extra horses. Informing him briefly that he had met with an accident, Sloan quickly selected a mount and swung astride, riding bareback to the spot where the roan had gone down. In a few minutes he transferred his saddle, and they were ready to push on.

Under no necessity now to follow every twist and turn of the wild band, the pair were able to pick their own trail. Selecting the easiest going, they gained rapidly on the horse hunters. Inside of twenty minutes they spied Lilholt and his men half a mile ahead, and almost at once Sam burst out, "There's Idaho! See how he keeps looking back! He's wondering how we'll take this—"

Pat's expression was bleak. "Stay away and pretend to ignore him," he warned. "I want him to forget us when things tighten up. That will be our chance."

They overtook the others as the mustangs were being hazed down into the canyon. Riding hard, they helped turn the band south as intended.

"Good work," Lilholt called, jogging close. "Where were you boys?"

Pat briefly indicated Sam's fresh horse. "Little accident—" he brushed the matter off.

Lilholt nodded. It was no more than was to be expected in this rough country. "Keep them moving!" was his parting cry.

The open canyon spread nearly a half-mile wide. Its sides were not high, and they had work making sure the mustangs drove straight on. Fortunately, the second group of horse hunters joined them, and they were able to stretch a ragged line of men across the mouth of the canyon while others guarded its broken slopes.

Whatever Towner's intentions toward Sam Sloan had been, he now kept his distance, assiduously helping to haze the wild bunch on. Pat kept a careful eye on his movements. Ahead of them the mustangs skimmed over the canyon floor like swallows, venting uneasy whistles of defiance and running sidewise as they turned their heads to look back at their pursuers. It was a stirring sight. There were duns, blacks, light bays and a number of roans in the bunch. Pat noted the colorful coat of a spirited yearling paint pony.

"How far down does this trap lay?" a man sang out.

"Couple miles, I judge," Lilholt sang out. "We'll see Gabe and the others first. When they turn the stuff up-slope we'll crowd in behind and push them hard."

A hawk, alarmed by the clatter of hoofs and the racing figures, sailed out from the cliff over the fleeing mustangs and very nearly ruined the hard work of the men. In a twinkling the wild herd broke and sought to scatter. It took desperate riding to prevent them from losing themselves in the maze of broken gullies or breaking back. The men dashed this way and that, yelling and waving their hats until the explosive stampede was quelled and the band thundered on.

Sam reined close to where Stevens was riding. "That could've been the break we were looking for, boy," he called across. "I could have grabbed Towner myself then."

Pat's headshake was curtly decisive. "Not yet," he
warned tightly. "Be ready when I give the sign, Sam. This
has got to go off like clockwork, and we'll want Ez in on
it, if possible."

The men were pushing the mustangs harder now, keeping them moving at a brisk run. With the lower canyon
apparently wide open for them, the wild ones raced on.
Rocky ledges and brush-tufted outcrops flashed past. The
mustangs sailed over a ten-foot wash without breaking
stride.

Suddenly a cry rang out. Stevens saw Gabe Marsh, Ezra
and the third rider break into view directly before the
fleeing herd. Their yells pealed, followed by the echoing
crack of guns. The headlong rush of the mustangs broke.
For a second it looked as if they might scatter in a dozen
directions, then the lead horses swerved, heading up the
canyon slope.

Marsh's stentorian bellow of triumph rang over the sage.
The leader vigorously waved the men on, urging them to
close in. As matters stood, they had only to press the
pursuit home, and the wild horses would inevitably pour
up over the low rise and slam into the trap.

Pat made a guarded signal to Sam. "Swing over and tip
Ez off!" He himself was jockeying for position behind
Idaho, intending to close in fast and collar the renegade.

The best time seemed to be just as the mustangs tipped
up over the rise of the saddle and headed into the trap
wings. The horse hunters were sure to be crowding them
close and would pay no heed to what went on in their rear.
Towner unconsciously abetted this plan by falling back.
But he was wary, shooting looks about as if taking stock
of the situation. Stevens saw Sam and Ezra unobtrusively
maneuvering to cover Idaho's confederates and take them
swiftly out of the game.

Up the sage-dotted slope dashed men and horses in a
rising uproar of clattering hoofs and yells. The crest,
behind which lay the trap, loomed just ahead. The first of
the mustangs topped out and passed from sight. Pat swept

a hard look about, noting the position of every man. Then he gave the Bar ES partners the signal for action.

As he did so, Pat was astounded to glimpse four mounted figures atop the ridge a matter of rods away from where the mustangs were streaming past. Paying no heed to the horses, the four headed downward toward the pursuing riders. It was plain at once that the attention of the newcomers was fastened squarely on one man, and that man was Idaho Towner.

"Hey! There's Ed Roman yonder," cried Sam harshly. "What's *he* doing here?"

Within seconds Pat and his friends saw the U.S. marshal and his deputies ram their mounts straight at Towner. The outlaw spotted them. He yanked his bronc to a halt, the horse rising on hind legs and pawing the air. Idaho hauled it down by main strength, whirled it around and slammed off in another direction.

It was done so quickly that Stevens was wholly unable to cut Towner off. Roman threw a shot over Idaho's head. "Haul up, Towner! We've got you cold," he bawled out harshly.

He spoke too soon. No one noticed Towner's cronies closing in until they cut across the posse's path. Instantly a tangle of dancing horses brought utter confusion. Curses rang out, orders were yelled which nobody heeded.

Idaho took full advantage of his opportunity. His bronc racing away, the burly outlaw flashed out of sight behind a rocky ledge. Pat hurled his mount that way, only to become entangled in thick matted brush. To his savage disgust, he was forced to rein up. Ez and Sam had no better luck.

Thanks to Marshal Roman's unwarranted interference at the critical moment, Idaho Towner had succeeded in making good his escape.

14.

THE minute he caught sight of Roman and his deputies, Gabe Marsh turned back. He rammed his mount close and grabbed the marshal by one arm, forcibly arresting his attention.

"What do you think you're up to here, mister?" he rapped out.

Roman tore away from his grasp, his sharp gaze raking the other man. "Never mind," he gave back roughly. "This doesn't concern you—"

"By God, it does, and I want you to know it!" Marsh refused to be put off. "Here we're putting in days of hard work for a few dollars, and you think you can plow right into the middle of it!"

Ignoring him for the moment, Roman yelled to his deputies. "Look lively, boys. Grab those clumsy fools that blocked our chance!" He waved in the direction of Idaho's friends, who were doing their best now to make their escape.

The deputies had already taken their cue, wheeling their ponies aside to cut off the fugitives. But the renegades were wily. Barnes reined behind a tall clump of brush, and Bart Lackey jumped his bronc down a precipitous ledge.

"Over here, Sam," called Stevens, plunging after Barnes. "He's got to make a break for the open!"

They raced out to close in on the fugitive. Trying to outmaneuver them, Barnes wheeled back. He made a miscalculation, however. Bursting out of the obscuring brush, the man found both Pat and Sam Sloan blocking his way. Throwing his gun up, he fired ineffectually and hurled his pony into the gap between them.

Sam made a frantic effort to cut him off. Too late for that, he strove desperately to throw an arm about Barnes as the latter plunged past. Even this was a failure. Sam had all he could do to keep from tumbling headlong out of the saddle.

Pat was cooler, wheeling to a stand. His Colt flashed up. At its crack Barnes vented a cry and fell backward over the cantle, his grip on the reins causing his mount to come to a plunging halt. As the animal reared up on its hindlegs, the renegade's grip relaxed, and he slid limply to the ground.

"You got him!" cried Sam. He managed to capture the riderless horse before it could race away.

Bart Lackey had been more fortunate than his companion. Cut off from the view of his pursuers for a critical ten seconds by the ledge from which he had jumped his horse, the renegade was already well away and going like the wind.

The possemen fired after him without effect. Using precious moments to descend the ledge without injury to their ponies, they raced after the fleeing man. But Lackey had a thousand-yard lead by the time they struck out in his wake. If they caught up with him at all, it would be only after a long hard chase. Idaho had long since disappeared over the bulge of the sage slope a quarter-mile away.

Seeing that his help was not needed in the chase, Pat swung to the ground. Barnes glared up implacably when he was rolled over. Stevens kicked his fallen gun away from his hand.

"Get up on your hocks," he grunted. "You've got a crease across your back, Barnes, but you're not killed by a long shot."

Looking vaguely surprised, the renegade sat up, wincing, then struggled to his feet. He was still sullen when Sam yanked his hands behind his back and tied them.

The mustangs and the horse hunters had moments ago

faded from sight over the crest of the saddle, leaving a brown haze of dust which the breeze whipped and eddied about. Remounting his pony, Pat looked across toward Marsh.

"I expect those broomtails are corralled by this time?" he called.

"No thanks to this hombre—" Gabe made an exasperated gesture toward the lawman.

While Sam was forcing the captured renegade back astride his bronc, Stevens rode forward to face Roman squarely. "Marshal," he began flatly. "I took a deputy's badge with the understanding that you were to leave me a free hand with Idaho Towner. You can explain now why it was necessary to barge into the middle of things just as I was about to grab my man!"

Roman regarded him dourly. "You took too long," he said. "I learned from young Majors and Durgen's girl that Towner was out here. Expected you'd be bringing him in during the next day or so—"

"Badge-toter, eh?" broke in Marsh suspiciously. "Are you admitting you rode in here wearing a badge, Stevens?" He was growing more incensed by the moment at what appeared to him a plain case of injustice.

"If you knew you were protecting a wanted man, I'd have something to say to you too," Roman snapped back before Pat found time to reply. "*Did* you know who Towner was, mister?"

"Yes, I know who he is!" Gabe was in full stride now, pounding a palm with his fist. "He was one of my horse hunters, and so is Stevens! When a man asks me for work, I don't ask him his pedigree. I don't need yours either, friend—you can be on your way. And I'll expect Stevens to get back to work too! So now you know!"

If Gabe threw all the authority at his command into these words, it was not enough to overawe these men. Pat brushed the command aside as if he had scarcely heard. "Sorry, Marsh. I'll be on Idaho's trail for a spell. As you say—but for Roman here, we might have had him on ice by now. And we'll be lucky if we don't lose him altogether!''

"Nonsense!" Gabe grew almost apoplectic. "We're about to lay hands on a nice pot of money, Stevens. The next big drive will do it. You can't turn your back on that for any man."

"Can't, eh? . . . Will our share add up to twenty-five hundred, Marsh?" Ezra broke in.

Gabe was taken aback. "I said you'd be working for wages," he returned tartly. "Why do you name any such figure?"

"Because that's the price on Towner's head right now," Ez told him. "Roman told us that, and we came out here after him. It was lying there for you to pick up, if you hadn't been so interested in horses. But do you blame us on that account?"

Marsh looked startled, much of his steam gone. Yet he was able to summon up indignation. "You could've told us that, Marshal, and had your man by now," he snapped.

Roman was unimpressed. "Where do you suppose Idaho would be if he saw me riding out here to tell you?" he retorted. "Waiting around to see what would happen?"

Gabe was about to fire out a heated response when one of the horse hunters came jogging over the ridge. Spotting Marsh, he let out a hail.

"Come on, Gabe! We got them nags penned in the corral all snug and tidy. Don't you want a look?"

Marsh turned his horse that way, but hesitated. "Law or no law, I'll be obliged if you'll pull out of here and leave us to our work, Marshal," he bit out.

Roman was looking at Sam's prisoner. "Don't worry," he growled. "Right now I'm taking this hombre in charge. Then I'll push along after my men." He turned. "What about you, Stevens?"

Pat regarded him levelly. "I'll give you an answer when you give me one." He spoke tightly. "Do we have a free hand with Towner from here on out, Roman—or do you think you can do better?"

It was put strongly, but the federal officer never batted

an eye. "Said I wanted you to run Idaho down, didn't I?" he countered coolly. "You're still carrying my badge—and he's gaining distance on you with every jump."

Pat's nod was curt. "Just so we understand each other. I don't expect to see Towner again today," he allowed. "He won't be back here, that's sure. We'll pick up our pack horse and be on our way. If you don't see us again, that'll be okay with us." It was notice in full that Roman was invited to ignore their activities till they had something to report.

"Just don't come back without Towner," was Roman's unyielding comment. Taking the reins of the renegade's horse, the marshal started away.

Stevens turned to Sam. "Get back to camp, you and Ez, and gather up our bed rolls," he directed. "We'll pick up Towner's sign and shove along."

The pair jogged off. Returning half an hour later leading the pack animal, they found Pat working out the outlaw's tracks a mile or two further down the canyon. There was no sign of Marshal Roman and his deputies.

"They rushed off in a sweat," Pat explained. "If they're lucky, they may grab Lackey. I wouldn't count on it."

Ezra scanned Idaho Towner's tracks in silence. Finally he spoke. "He didn't make any try at breaking trail here," he remarked. 'We can look for that next."

He was right. Within another mile, Towner's sign began to fade on rocky ground. Ez picked it up again and again, but each time this proved harder of accomplishment. Pat finally called a halt.

"That's enough, Ez," he ruled. "At the rate Idaho was going, it's plain we won't overhaul him this way. I was only wondering if his tracks gave some clue to which way he was heading."

Sam laughed scornfully at this. "You don't think he was really going backward, do you?" he gibed.

Paying no attention, Ez looked inquiringly at Pat. Stevens waved a decisive hand. "We're wasting time here by the minute," he averred. "There can't be much question where Towner would head first of all."

Sam sobered. "Where's that?"

"He'll soon figure it out that Majors tipped Roman off to where he was hiding," Pat said. "I didn't want Roman to catch on too fast—but knowing Idaho, I'd say he was on his way to paying his respects at Durgen's store."

"By gravy, you're right!" Ez at once dropped his trailing. "We can't waste any more time. Let's get back there fast, boy."

They turned back, taking the most direct route across the wild Uncompahgre wasteland. It was impossible, however, to avoid the rugged canyons and knife-edge ridges, and despite their best efforts, they lost time. It was late the following afternoon before the swell of the San Rafael hills rose before them.

Pushing steadily upward, they came within sight of the isolated store as dusk was lowering. Bobby Durgen came hurrying out on the porch as they drew near.

"Pat, I'm so glad you've come!" she exclaimed in an unmistakable tone of distress.

Delaying his question until he dismounted and approached the steps, Stevens asked, "What's the trouble now, Bobby?"

"It's Kit," she all but wailed. "He's been gone all day. He—promised faithfully to be back in an hour or two, and I can't imagine what could have happened!"

Pat frowned, climbing the steps to stand beside Bobby while Ez and Sam quietly looked after the weary horses. "Majors was told to stick around here and keep an eye on things. What drew him off?" he queried soberly.

"The store was broken into and robbed last night," the girl brought out with a rush. "I tried to tell Marshal Roman he was making a mistake to leave—"

"What was taken?" Pat interrupted swiftly. "Were you able to tell?"

Her nod was distracted. "A large quantity of food supplies—and I think several boxes of ammunition. At least, that's what I've discovered missing so far. Our few dollars in cash weren't where the robber could find them."

Pat grunted, not at all surprised. "Go on, Bobby."

"They apparently broke in the corner window—whoever

it was. Kit discovered the door standing ajar this morning," she explained. "Father was furious when he heard. We—can hardly afford such losses. Dad insisted that we check at once to learn what was missing. He helped." She clasped her hands together, revealing her tension and dismay. "The shortage ran to at least a hundred dollars."

Sam and Ez returned in time to hear the last of this. The pudgy man whistled. "How do you figure that, Stevens?" he put in gruffly.

Pat ignored this, his eyes fastened on the girl.

"Kit was—angry too," she continued. "He looked around outside and found what he said were plain tracks. I begged him to wait for someone, but he was determined to follow the tracks at least a way's. He promised to be very careful."

They moved inside as the darkness thickened. Pat pulled down the hanging coal-oil lamp and lit it. It swung briefly on its chain after he released it, and the swaying shadows seemed to emphasize the ominous quiet. It was Ezra who finally spoke.

"Idaho Towner, like as not," he said grimly.

Pat's nod left little room for doubt. "If it meant he was getting ready to pull out of the country, a hundred dollars would be cheap enough. But those tracks that were so easy to read—" He shook his head.

Bobby anxiously studied his dour expression. "What does it mean, Pat? You don't think Kit is still trailing Idaho Towner somewhere in the hills?"

The partners read Pat's thought quickly enough. If Idaho left a plain trail following the store robbery, it could very well be because he wanted to be followed. It was entirely possible that even now young Majors was a prisoner in the ruthless outlaw's hands; but Stevens had no intention of adding to Bobby's fears by spelling this out.

"What does your father say about it?" he changed the subject.

"Of course he appreciates Kit's efforts to help. I'm afraid he doesn't—believe it will come to much." Her tone was apologetic. "Dad seems to think we're both too young to know what we're doing."

Pat turned abruptly toward the door leading into the living quarters. "I want a word or two with Durgen. Can I see him?"

"He'll be as relieved as I am to see you, Pat." Bobby led the way into the kitchen, where old Ducks was sitting in his chair near the stove. The old man looked up testily.

"You, Stevens?" he barked. "Why ain't you never around when you're needed?"

Pat greeted him civilly. "Sorry to hear of this robbery, Durgen. You seem to be having a run of bad luck, and no mistake."

"Well—that Majors kid was supposed to be on guard against such things as that," rasped Durgen. "He ain't very dependable though. I'm thinking seriously of giving up the store and moving into town," he added bleakly.

"But, Dad!" cried Bobby. "We couldn't know this was going to happen. Right now I'm afraid Kit has gone too far trying to help us."

Old Ducks snorted. "You kids." He turned toward Stevens. "Only this afternoon I had to stop her from following Majors—wherever he's rushed off to. I still think she's got some crazy idea in her head. I leave it to you how much that would help!"

Pat shook his head, directing a frown at the girl. "Why didn't you tell me that?" he chided. "Whatever you do, Bobby, don't ever make such a foolish move. Because that would be exactly what Idaho Towner was hoping for."

15.

BOBBY blanched as the outlaw's name came out at last, confirming her gravest suspicions. "Pat, something *must* be done!" she pleaded. "There's no need to hide from me that Kit must be in great danger."

"All right," Pat spoke bluntly. "If you're sure of that, you must know it'll do no good to follow his example and go rushing around. Just let me handle this. Will you do that?"

She nodded uncertainly. "But what can you do—?"

"Not a thing till daylight. If I know Towner, he's not stupid enough to stick around after robbing the place—or any other crook, for that matter," he added seeing her dismay.

"It *was* Idaho, wasn't it?" she whispered.

"Not so fast." Sure as he was, he was not prepared to commit himself. "If we figure it that way, we'll know the worst we can be up against, and there won't be any ugly surprises."

"What'll you do, Stevens?" Durgen broke in brusquely.

Pat shrugged. "We'll make sure nothing of the kind happens tonight—not that I expect it will. In the morning Ez will see what he can make of those tracks."

Bobby started. "Oh! You must all be starving," she exclaimed apologetically. "I'll have supper ready directly."

Following a hearty meal, Pat brought Durgen and Bobby up to date. He related how they had found Idaho Towner hiding with the horse hunters, and how they had maneuvered to corner the outlaw without a slip, only to have Marshal Roman ruin their plans by riding into the scene at the critical moment.

Following every word, old Ducks revealed by his vehemence that, confined as he was to his invalid's chair, he still considered himself a man of action. "Dang that Towner anyhow! He'll keep fooling around, and I'll be his finish yet!" he whipped out hoarsely.

"But what can he want here?" interjected Bobby nervously. "Can he still be hoping to eliminate the witnesses to his killing of Kit's father?"

Pat saw that she dreaded the answer, but did not try to brush the question aside. "Something like that must have been in his mind," he admitted. "On the other hand, Ed Roman unquestionably poses the biggest threat against him. Towner already has a couple of killings chalked up to his credit over at Rocky Ford. If it was me, I'd be making tracks for Montana or Mexico without losing time about it. And it could be that idea will finally percolate through Idaho's thick head."

Pat's frankness reassured the girl a little. "If Towner stole supplies for a long trip, we can at least hope that he lost Kit somewhere on the trail. Kit *may* simply have followed too far to return tonight. But—shouldn't we expect him to show up by tomorrow morning?"

Pat would take no part in such idle speculations. "Tomorrow will tell us that. Whether he does or not won't help us overhaul Idaho. Shall we turn in?" he said, ending the talk.

They bedded down as before, with one man outside to alert them at the first disturbance and another in the store. As Pat fully expected, the night passed without incident.

Bobby was awake and moving about before dawn; she quickly prepared breakfast. Durgen did not appear. The Powder Valley trio ate in silence, and first light saw them saddling up. It did not escape them that the girl came again and again to the porch, her worried glance sweeping the open. Majors had not put in an appearance during the small hours, nor did he now.

"We taking the pack pony this time?" asked Sam as they made ready to start.

Pat vetoed the idea. "We won't go that far—and if we do, we won't want a drag on us."

Ready at last, Ezra walked around the store studying the beaten ground. He picked up Kit's tracks and spotted the trail the puncher had followed. Waving the others after him, he set off on foot, swiftly reading the signs which Pat and Sam were hard put to see at all. A few minutes later, when there was less chance of stray tracks obscuring the trail, he mounted.

A mile farther on Ezra spoke. "I don't like it, Stevens." He shook his grizzled head. "Towner had one man with him. They picked up a pack animal somewhere. Twice they passed up a good chance to break trail—and from *his* tracks, Majors never noticed that."

"Tolling him on, eh?" Pat was terse. "Keep going, Ez. We'll see if we can learn what happened."

Before midmorning they came to a spot where the trail ran under the rim of a broken rock ledge and where a horse had danced about. There were other tracks at the spot. It all made plain reading. Ez grimly pointed out the evidence.

"They you are. They rode past here, circled back on that ledge, and either bent a gun on young Kit when he came by, or dabbed a rope on him."

Pat flashed a quick look about the spot. "Spread out and cast around here, boys," he directed. "We'll make sure Towner didn't knock Kit off on the spot and tumble him in the brush."

After a twenty-minute search, they breathed easier. Whatever had been done with Majors, he had not been murdered and left behind. "Makes you wonder just what Towner's game is," commented Sam.

"You reckon he figures to hold Kit as a hostage, Stevens?" Ez asked.

Pat refused to make a guess. "He's got some object in mind, that's sure. I get the idea all this is some kind of game to Idaho."

"He's a natural born schemer," Ez agreed. "And he's

over his mad now. He can always finish Majors off once he makes up his mind to it.''

"That's the point," Pat thrust in. "The sooner we block whatever his game is, the better Kit's chance of coming out of this alive."

Ez began picking up the trail of the outlaws once more. Pat rode close beside him, while Sam dawdled along in the rear, obviously pondering. "Shake a leg there, slow-poke," his lanky partner threw over his bony shoulder.

Sam came trotting forward, his face bleak. "Mighty sure of yourself, ain't you?" he fired out. Then, making sure he had his companions' attention, Sloan threw his bomb. "Idaho tolled Majors plumb into his hands with no trouble at all," he drawled. "What gives you the superior notion he's not doing the same thing to us?"

This gave them pause. Stevens weighed the possibility and curtly dismissed it. "I wish he would try that! . . . We're a mite different from Kit Majors, for one thing. To get anywhere with us, Sam, he'd have to wipe the three of us out. Idaho's too cagey to tackle that.''

Another twenty minutes demonstrated the improbability of any such bold attempt, as the trail of the quarry faded out on rocky ground. Ez located it again a hundred yards farther on, but thereafter it was plain that Idaho was taking pains now to lose his tracks.

Ez laboriously worked out the outlaw's sign for another half-mile, then lost it altogether. He kept trying to pick it up again until Pat finally called him off. "We're wasting time again, Ez." He gauged the sun, halfway down the western sky. "Time to get back there to the store."

As they turned back, the same sobering thought came to them all: that if Idaho was indeed bent on pulling out of the country, Kit's body might even now be lying some-where along the trail ahead.

Stevens clung stubbornly to his belief that such was not the case. "No—he aims to use Majors for some purpose or other," he insisted. "It's up to us to figure out what."

Cutting straight across the hills, one more hour brought them within sight of the store again. It stood out against

the evening sky, lonely and deserted as ever. Pat drew up
on a rise to scan the horizon.

"Come on, boy," called Sam. "We'll see if anybody's
been around while we were away. Maybe Roman's come
back—"

But Pat still sat motionless in his saddle. Ez turned to
see what interested him. For a moment he saw nothing;
then his single slitted eye fixed.

"What *is* that?" His tone was sharp. "Some hombre
forking his bronc there on yonder ridge—?"

Pat gazed a moment longer before responding. "Too far
away to be sure. It looks like somebody was keeping a
watch over there till he saw us. . . . Let's look into this!"

He rammed his mount that way, and the others quickly
followed. They saw the man on the distant rise linger, then
abruptly urge his pony forward, horse and rider disappearing over the brow of the ridge.

"He spotted us," Sam cried out. "Did you make out
who it was, Stevens?"

Pat had not. "I'll make one guess who's interested in
our movements though," he threw back.

They drove their horses forward at their best speed. Ten
minutes took them to the ridge on which the mysterious
rider had appeared. Topping out at a point where his tracks
showed, they gazed down the long undulating sea of brush
beyond.

"There he goes!" Sam pointed out a tiny bobbing dot a
mile away. "We can nail him easy!" He would have
pushed on immediately, but Pat held up an arresting hand.

"Hold it, Sam! This looks too much like the caper they
pulled on Kit—"

"By grab!" Ezra wheeled back, his hatchet face keenly
alert. "You're right at that. . . . Is that buzzard trying to
draw us away from the store?"

Pat had already turned back. "That we're about to find
out." With the partners in his wake, he made straight for
the Durgen place. No word was spoken as they hurried
forward, but their eyes were busy. The isolated building

told them nothing as they drew near. Stevens drew rein before the porch steps. "Bobby!" he called out.

There was no response. There was, in fact, an ominous silence hanging over the place.

Sliding to the ground, Pat bounded up the steps. He thrust the door back, stepped inside, and turned back with a sober expression. "Nobody in the store," he announced.

"But old Durgen's pretty nearly got to be here. We'll see what he says—"

"If he *is* around," interjected Sam, trying to remain levelheaded. "The girl could have taken him to see a sawbones, you know."

Followed by the others, Pat pushed on through the store to the inner rooms. As they reached the kitchen a querulous screech came to their ears from Durgen's tiny bedroom. They heard the bang of his cane.

"What now? Who is that?" From his tone, old Ducks was ablaze with indignation. "Are you back, girl? What's the meaning of all this?"

They burst in to find the old man sitting in his chair beside the window. His fierce eyes flared up as they fell on these bulky masculine forms instead of his daughter. "You three again, hey?"

"Alone, are you? Where's Bobby?" asked Pat directly.

"She's gone—that's where she is," Ducks bawled furiously. "Where in hell were you birds when it happened, Stevens? It's the same old story again!"

"All right, simmer down," Pat said brusquely. "The quicker you tell us what happened here, oldtimer, the sooner we can do something about it." If he expected the worst he managed to keep it out of his voice.

"One of Idaho Towner's rats showed up an hour or two ago," the old fellow jerked out. "It was that Lackey—I seen him ride past the window here. I yelled to that girl to lock the doors. She didn't hear me—or she wasn't quick enough. Lackey got inside. I heard them talking together."

"What were they saying?"

Old Ducks brushed this aside impatiently. "Couldn't catch a word of it!"

"There's no doubt about it being Lackey, I don't suppose?" Pat demanded thinly.

Durgen snorted. "If there was, I wouldn't say it was him! He's been here before with Towner, holding the horses and toadying around. . . . It was him all right!"

It was the worst news they could have expected. "What happened then?"

Old Ducks went apoplectic, banging his cane savagely. "She went off with him! Would you believe it? He gave her a song and dance about young Majors, likely, and she fell for it!"

Sam was sympathetic. "Nothing you could do about that, was there?"

Durgen's jaw jutted implacably. "I sure tried," the old man said. "I took a shot at him with this as he was riding off with her." From under the blanket covering his useless legs he whipped a murderous-looking, battered old cap-and-ball pistol. "Think I winged the buzzard too—but he didn't stop."

The trio exchanged glances. It looked bad. But Pat was intent on learning all he could. "Didn't you hear anything they said, Durgen?"

The old man growled, forced to repeat that he had not caught a single word. He went off on a rambling diatribe against Idaho, which Stevens as quickly cut short.

"Take a look around the store, will you, Sam?" he ordered briefly.

Ezra and Sloan turned back to comply while Pat continued his questioning of old Ducks. The old man told him that he had seen no sign of Idaho himself, nor any other member of the owlhoot crowd aside from Lackey.

They were still talking when Sam came hurrying back, a crumpled paper fluttering in his hand. "Look, Stevens. We found this on a corner of the counter," he exclaimed.

Pat grabbed the paper and stepped to the window, holding it to the light. It was a corner of soiled and much creased newspaper bearing crude writing on its margin. For a moment he could make nothing of the faint, smudged letters. Then the sense of it began to emerge:

MAM—WER BAD OFF FR COFFE FECH US A FEW
LBS AN I COUD BE TAWKED INTO TURNIN MA-
JOR LOOS—

BY U NO HU

Pat read the message aloud in an emotionless voice.
"You know who," he repeated grimly. "That's Idaho's
trademark, as plain as we'll ever need it."

Durgen groaned, all his fiery defiance evaporated now.
"She *would* go overboard for that Majors boy. Towner
was smart enough to figure on that. What could he want of
her, Stevens? Is he that crazy to get back at me?" He
seemed to dread the response, his eyes pleading.

Pat was slow to answer. Certain as he was, he was
reluctant to deal the helpless old man this final blow. But
Durgen was too shrewd to be put off with evasions.

"There's only one possible reason, Durgen. I won't
lie about this. As he sees it, Towner's got his hands on
the only living witness to the murder of Lyte Majors.
Sorry—but that's how it is."

16.

DUCKS DURGEN'S fury had burned out at last, leaving only despair. He knew he was hearing the truth.

"You're right," he muttered. "Bobby and Kit won't be back unless somebody goes after them." His headshake was dull, his fierce old eyes lackluster. "I haven't the money to pay anyone, Stevens."

"We won't let this pass," Pat quickly reassured him. "Take it easy, Durgen. . . . For that matter, I expect to take my pay out of Towner's hide." He turned to Sam. "Tell Ez to make sure we have enough grub for several days."

"Sure thing." The stocky man headed back into the store.

Pat was silent for a while, peering absently out the window. His next question revealed the direction of his thoughts. "Durgen, you must know this range pretty well," he began. "Where would Idaho take those youngsters—for a guess?"

"Don't know." Old Ducks brooded gloomily. "This is no time for guessing, boy. You got to track that wolf down and smash him!"

There was no argument there. But Stevens knew that any stray fact about this strange country he was able to pick up might have a direct bearing on the speed with which it could be done. He was still putting his queries, without much result, when Sam came back.

"All set, Stevens. We can shove off when you're

130

ready. . ." He broke off, and it was plain that what he said next came hard. "Leaving Durgen here alone, are we? I'll—stick around and keep an eye on things, if you say the word."

"No," Pat replied at once. "We'll move fast, and I want you along, Sam." He regarded the merchant. "What about it, Durgen? Can you look after yourself if we lock the place up and go?"

Durgen made a violent gesture with his cane. "What are you waiting for?" he demanded. "And don't do no locking up. If somebody comes, they can wait on themselves. I've run into this before."

Pat nodded. "Marshal Roman may be back any time. But we won't wait."

They saw that Durgen had a pitcher of water and such food as he was likely to need near at hand, and then went out to the yard. With the horses ready and waiting, Ezra was again puzzling out the tracks. He pointed out the way he thought Bobby and the treacherous Lackey had gone.

"What about that hombre we saw on the way in?" asked Ez as they mounted. "Reckon we'd save time by fogging after him?"

Pat waved this aside. "As I read it, that was a ruse to stall us and give Lackey more time to get the girl away. We'll stick to her trail. It's bound to lead straight to Idaho Towner in the end."

Evening was not far off when they started. Ez led the way at a brisk pace, keenly aware that even a mile or two gained might make the difference between success and failure. They had no trouble reading the trail, which still ran south, when the shades of night lowered over the range, making it impossible to follow it farther with any certainty.

Camping beside a willow-bordered creek, they ate a meager supper. It was early when they turned in and they were astir before first light in the morning. They saddled up and jogged out to pick up the trail afresh, purpose in their every movement. This could be the day.

Ez picked up the sign at once. An hour later the

southward-looping trail of the two saddled horses they were following swung east. Ezra glanced up and about, scanning their surroundings. The dark swell of the mountains loomed ahead.

"Lackey's making for the San Juans," he announced.

Pat nodded, measuring the ragged peaks rising into the morning sky. "It figures. With Ed Roman chasing him out of the Uncompahgre, Towner will try to lose himself in these wild San Juan canyons—and the right man could pretty nearly succeed," he added.

Sam continued to gaze about with interest as they worked up into the foothills. "Right on the edge of mining country, ain't we?" he asked, taking in the cedar clumps replacing the endless sage, and the aspen groves on the steep slopes ahead.

"It used to be," Pat said. "At least there was considerable mining activity through the San Juans a few years ago. But a mine had to be rich to avoid shutting down—too hard to get to," he explained.

In the shadow of the lofty peaks they toiled upward, still following the trail. Toward midday the sun, high above the granite shoulders, beat directly down on them. Despite the steady wind roaring through the pine tops, it was hot work, but no one complained; they didn't even stop to eat, but grabbed a bite in the saddle.

In a rocky hollow overlooking the gray rolling plains Ez pointed out where three more shod ponies had turned in to join the pair they were trailing. "Would that be Idaho?" queried Sam, his voice sharp.

"They may have planned to meet here." Pat's tone was steady. "Could you say how long ago, Ez?"

The lanky tracker did not answer immediately. He shrugged. "Can't pin it down. Sometime during the night or early morning."

"How do you know that?" challenged Sam.

Ezra showed where a horse had brushed through a sage clump that it had not seen in the dark—it would have missed it in the daylight. Sloan grunted. Never yet had he managed to match his partner in the skill of reading trail.

"All right—shove off." Pat waved them on. "They won't wait for us."

Sam hesitated uneasily. "Should we look around here first?" he began.

Pat read his thought. His headshake was curt. "Idaho wouldn't have waited this long if he intended to finish off those young folks in a hurry," he gave his opinion. "He'll play his cat-and-mouse game with them first. That may be our chance to draw up on him while there's still time."

It sounded ominous. They thrust on without further delay. "Towner must be pretty sure of himself," Sam remarked. "He doesn't seem to be trying to shake us off this time. Didn't take him long to do it before."

"Shut up, fat stuff." The secret anxiety he shared with Sam made Ezra taut. "No time to be looking for complications now."

The tracks they followed wound steadily deeper into the mountains; they skirted canyons now and rode in and out of the shadow of tall cliffs. It was no surprise to see a wolf warily cross the trail some distance ahead, investigating the strange sign of shod horses. Shortly thereafter a startled elk crashed through the dense spruce.

They made better time across a sloping, pine-roofed plateau. Here, there was a cool breeze, laden with the scent of conifer and sage. But the occasional clumps of cedar and the scattered rocks studding the plateau kept them alert and cautious; more than once Stevens or Sam circled ahead, warding off possible ambush, while Ezra doggedly worked out a trail.

In an open space at the upper edge of the plateau, they found signs that the renegades had drawn up briefly, their horses stamping, while they probably discussed their future course. Pat delayed here, casting about the spot with care. Suddenly he swung out of the saddle, bending down to snatch some object up from the ground.

"What is that?" barked Sam.

It was an inch or two of ribbon, obviously torn from Bobby Durgen's dress and dropped here as a sign. Fortunately, the outlaws had not spotted it. Ez nodded approval.

"Smart girl," he growled. "Shows she ain't lost her spunk yet."

The discovery lent urgency to their movements. Still the trail of the quarry revealed no serious attempt at concealment, curving down across a wide, shallow valley beyond the plateau. Here the pines gave place to willow, with fringes of alder marking the shallow water courses. Tufted with buffalo grass, the ground was soft enough to show plainly every hoofprint of the horses, and they made good time.

"Ought to be drawing up on them at this rate," Sam ventured at length.

Ez shot a glance across at Pat. "Think maybe Towner's got a hideout up here in some high valley, Stevens? Nothing much else to draw a man up here under them peaks."

Pat lifted his head to scan the lofty San Juans, soaring sheer into the blue above them. A faint shrug stirred his broad shoulders. "Idaho could be making for some high pass," he conjectured. "If he aimed to put plenty of miles behind him, that would explain this plain trail he's been leaving."

It only made the need for haste more pressing. The trail they followed wound down through a tortuous gorge and broken rockslides before angling once more across a steep pine-clothed slope. The only passage here was a faint deer trail. Idaho seemed to have worked steadily around the flank of a small peak.

They rode hastily up each succeeding ridge, gazing alertly over the crest for a sight of the quarry. Oddly enough, when the warning came that they were drawing close at last, it was at a point where dense pine cut off their view.

It was Ez who held up an arresting hand at the edge of a rocky dyke; motionless, he listened keenly. The others drew rein. After an endless moment the steady breeze wafted to them the faint, unmistakable clatter of rocks on the hidden trail below.

"Horses?" muttered Sam.

Ez nodded. "A deer might make that racket—for a

second. Only some stupid rider would keep it up. . . . We got to be careful we don't do the same thing.''

They thrust forward, straining to draw up on the party ahead. From minute to minute Stevens sought to catch the sound of unguarded voices. But either the wind was wrong, or the outlaws were exercising caution.

Twenty minutes later the way led to the lip of another high, shallow valley ringed about with fluttering aspen groves. They were still unable to make out the figures they were so anxious to see, yet there seemed little doubt they were on the right track: only minutes ago some half dozen shod horses had passed that way. Ez paused to study their surroundings from a high vantage point.

"We can drop over the rim of this valley and circle ahead—if we're quick enough," he announced. "You aiming to close in on Towner, or watch him a while, or what?''

Pat was undecided at the moment. "It might be smart to tag along and look their camp over tonight.'' He gauged the sun, still only a couple of hours past midday. "I would like to make sure exactly what we're up against, though. . . .'' Then, swiftly, he made up his mind. "We'll close in and look that bunch over. Could be we can figure out from their actions how much time we've got.''

Abandoning the trail, they worked over the edge of the valley and rode down its length as swiftly as rough conditions permitted. To avoid making any noise, they kept the broncs on soft ground at every possible opportunity. Two miles farther on they cautiously turned toward the valley's lower reaches, where they could expect to bisect the trail of the oncoming outlaws. The pine clumps thinned, and clearings opened out ahead. Ez was in the lead now, advancing with wary deliberation.

He drew rein behind a ragged rock pile and peered out. Pat and Sam watched him tensely. Suddenly the faint thud of hoofs and the jingle of curb chains came to their ears. Ezra stiffened in his saddle.

Unable to wait any longer, Sloan thrust forward. "What do you see, Ez?'' he whispered.

Ez jerked his gaunt chin forward, tipping his black flatbrim back and scratching his grizzled head. "Take a look at that," he invited guardedly.

Through a gap in the alders they saw Idaho Towner's confederate, Lackey, driving a small band of four or five saddleless horses ahead of him. Idaho was not with him—nor Kit Majors—nor the girl. As near as they could see from where they were, Lackey was entirely alone. Sam fought his rising alarm. "Where in heck is the rest of 'em?" he whipped out under his breath. "Are they following after—?" As he spoke, he knew better. The trail behind the steadily traveling renegade was devoid of any sign of life.

Pat abruptly understood why they had heard no sound of voices. His mouth tightened. "Lackey's alone, boys," he declared flatly. "I don't know how he did it—but Idaho's tricked us again." He waved toward the renegade herding the horses along. "There's the reason for that plain trail!"

Ezra was sternly practical. "So what now, boy. Shall we grab this bird and wring his tail—or blast him down and have done with it?"

Pat quickly mapped out a plan. "You and I will swing ahead and bag Lackey while Sam lays back to watch the trail—just in case. Fire a shot, Sam, if Idaho *should* show up all of a sudden!" But he didn't sound as if he expected it.

Sloan watched them strike off through the brush and then selected a spot from which he could watch the back trail without being seen.

Ez and Pat were barely in time to block Lackey from turning down into a wild canyon that would have guarded him from approach for several miles. Working swiftly ahead of the little cavalcade, the pair drew up behind scattered boulders until the quarry came clattering close. They thrust into full view then at a distance of fifty feet, their guns trained on Lackey before he was aware of their presence.

"Just reach as high as you think is safe, Lackey," Pat called out.

Taken wholly by surprise, Lackey jerked his hands into the air. "What do you want of me, Stevens?"

"Go get his gun, Ez," Pat directed.

Lackey pretended dismay. "You got to help me hold these horses," he protested vehemently.

Pat waved this aside sternly. "Let them go," he tossed at Ez. "They've served Towner's purpose. . . . Where *is* Idaho, Lackey? And where did you drop Bobby Durgen off?" he barked.

Lackey measured him sullenly and shrugged. "Ain't seen Towner," he evaded, ignoring the query about the girl.

Pat studied him. "You're dumber than I thought. Where would you *say* Idaho was—at a guess?" he pressed.

"Talk away, mister. You can't get anything out of me I don't know."

"Maybe not." Stevens was markedly dry. "But old Durgen saw you pack the girl away from the store—just remember that. If anything happens to her, it's dollars to doughnuts a jury says you'll swing!"

But Lackey stubbornly refused to talk, his hard mouth clamped shut.

17.

SAM SLOAN came riding forward while Stevens was still trying to extract a crumb or two of information from Bart Lackey. "Nobody else coming," the stocky man announced. "What does Lackey say?"

Pat's smile was mirthless. "Mighty little."

Sam's beady eyes narrowed. "Shall I persuade him a little?"

"No—" Moved by no false impulse of humanity, Pat was merely practical. "We might do it. But it'll waste time we might not have to spare." He pointed back at the way they had come. "The answer lies back there somewhere."

"Sure of that, are you?"

Pat noted the wariness with which Lackey waited for his answer. The look on the renegade's face erased all his doubts. He nodded.

"We know Bobby was with this buzzard till Towner met them somewhere along the trail," he said. "Probably Idaho rigged this cute deal to make us think they were all together until we were tolled away past the turnoff. Well, it worked. We'll have to turn back till we pick up his sign again."

Ezra scowled at Lackey. "We'll have to tote this rat along with us. I better tie his busy little hands—"

They waited while Lackey's wrists were bound at his back. The renegade watched them uneasily until Ez turned his pony around and gave it a starting slap. "Jog along, you," he growled.

Trotting a few yards ahead as they started off, Lackey kept looking back with guarded interest. From his manner, Pat did not believe the man found any reason to hope for rescue along the way he had come. Having broken his trail, Idaho was probably now increasing the distance between himself and pursuit.

Following the trail which had brought them here, the trio were careful to keep a watch on all sides, hoping to spot the point at which Towner had cunningly turned off. The miles dropped behind, the sun began slanting down the sky, and still they had found nothing of interest. It was Sloan who discovered that the renegade captive was lagging along deliberately.

"Get a move on there, Lackey," he burst out. "We won't waste no time on you."

The owlhoot gave him a sullen glare. "I could do better with my hands free," he whined. "I didn't ask for this."

"You're asking for it now," roared Ez, glowering at him. "Just don't be surprised when you get it!"

Lackey treated them to a display of wrathful indignation, but they did not have to urge him again to mend his pace.

Half an hour later Ez shook his head in puzzlement. Nowhere had he or his companions noted a place where Idaho's trail branched.

"I don't get it," Ez grumbled. "All it would take is some spot where the broncs followed along a ledge or even some big rock. We know the girl came partway because we picked up that chunk of ribbon she dropped."

Listening, Lackey suddenly stiffened at these words. He said nothing, pretending to look away, yet he must have felt the noose closing around his neck. For the moment, however, Stevens was intent on something else.

"You think Bobby could have been hoisted off her bronc and then shoved on afoot?" he queried Ez.

"Come to think of it, I did spot saddle marks on a couple of them ponies Lackey was hazing along," Sam broke in. "But what became of the saddles?"

"Hid in the brush," growled Ez shortly.

It offered a fresh possibility to pursue. Observing that Lackey alertly followed every word spoken, Pat grew interested. "Towner may even have young Majors with him," he speculated. "And the girl makes three. If they set off afoot, either they didn't figure to go too far—or Idaho had fresh broncs waiting."

Ez put his finger on the flaw in this reasoning. "We could spend a week looking for a trail like that, Stevens, and not find it."

Haste appeared to have dropped from Stevens completely. He gazed about the welter of peaks and canyons surrounding them, and his straight lips opened and shut again without speech.

"What are you up to now, boy?" rasped Sam abruptly. "Catching flies?"

Pat seemed not to have heard the gibe. "I'm remembering what Majors told me about this country," he returned mildly. He stared at the various minor peaks visible from this point, and indicated one. "Isn't that Horse Fly Mountain?"

Failing to understand, Sam shrugged his disgust. Ez was more deliberate, scrutinizing the rugged spur with his single eye. "Reckon it is—"

Pat nodded his satisfaction. "Kit said they made a gold strike or two on Horse Fly, and there was considerable mining activity there a number of years ago. He said there was an abandoned mining town on the south slope."

Ez revealed quickening interest. "I remember that. You Bet, he called it. It can't be too many miles from here, either."

Pat glanced thoughtfully at Lackey. "What about that, Bart? Where would you say You Bet lies from here?"

"Never heard of the place," the renegade answered.

Ez snorted. "I'll bet you didn't! Not since Idaho told you where to meet him, anyway."

"What are you talking about?" blustered the other man. "I ain't seen Idaho since you and Roman chased him out of Gabe Marsh's camp. And I don't expect to!"

"You're right about that last anyhow," Sam assured

him thinly. "I suppose you didn't see Ducks Durgen's girl either!"

"She insisted on following me away from the store," Lackey brought out unblushingly after a moment's thought. "I finally managed to shake her—"

Pat brushed this pointless bickering aside. "Towner was mighty careful to rob Durgen's store of supplies," he said. "He must have been planning to go where grub is hard to find. We'll take a look at You Bet."

That suited the grizzled partners. Turning away from the profitless trail, they made directly for Horse Fly Mountain. The way led down into and out of a rugged canyon and up across rocky slopes where the horses found hard going. Their captive complained bitterly, but a killing look from Ezra persuaded him that there was no recourse.

It was late afternoon now; shadows gathered in the lower depths, but high on the flank of the peak it was still bright. No one, with the possible exception of Lackey, knew precisely where You Bet was located, but Kit Majors had said positively that it lay on the south side of the peak.

"We could be on the wrong mountain," muttered Sam, gazing over the bleak, empty prospect.

Pat thrust on, showing a serenity he was far from feeling. They could not afford a mistake now. Every passing hour made Kit's and Bobby's situation more precarious.

A sweeping view across the broad lower slopes showed only the desolate rocks and jutting crags. But a few minutes later, as he went around an outthrust shoulder of granite, Sloan sang out. As the others came up, he pointed out a mine dump clinging to the raw slant of the mountain a quarter-mile away.

"This is Horse Fly, all right," he growled his relief. "Now where's the big city?"

Working around giant fragments of rock balanced precariously on the shattered flank of the peak, they advanced slowly. Noting a ragged gash that sliced through the mountain shoulder like a shallow canyon, Stevens waved them that way. It was a hard climb for the straining horses, but finally they approached the canyon's lower edge.

Halting, with his head barely above the rocky crest, Pat took a cautious look over and down. He heard Ezra's grunt of gratification, and nodded. "This is it," he said.

A thousand yards or more down the canyon they saw a jumble of weathered, tumbledown frame buildings. No two were on precisely the same level; some appeared ready to slide into the gulf at the slightest disturbance; and if You Bet had ever boasted a main street, it must have been one of the shortest on record.

A mine dump or two clung to the steep slope above town. No evidence of activity was to be seen anywhere. There was no glass in the gaping windows; a broken wagon frame and a few pieces of rusted machinery lay about. They would have to search diligently to find any life whatever in the abandoned place.

Pat was far from trusting this appearance of desertion. "If Towner's here, and we tip him off that we're closing in, he'll turn on those youngsters in a flash," he said. "The question is, how to get into town without being spotted—"

"It'll be dusk in another hour or so," suggested Sam.

But Stevens refused to wait. "Another hour may be too late," he pointed out. "We don't know if Idaho is even here. I won't take the chance of guessing wrong." His eyes ran slowly over the slopes leading down toward town. "We can't ride in there—but one man may be able to make it on foot," he mused.

"What about Lackey here?" Ez asked. "One yelp out of him, and it'll give our whole game away." His baleful look said that he wished the renegade would try it.

Pat nodded. "You and I will stay here with Lackey while Sam makes a try at reaching town. . . . Sneak down through the rocks," he directed Sloan, "and don't show yourself there in You Bet any more than you have to."

Sam was ready to try anything. "Shall I grab Towner if I get the chance?"

"You won't." Pat was terse. "Your job is to make sure he's there—and don't let him know it. Try and find out where Kit and Bobby are too, if you can. But don't pull any crazy rescue stunts by yourself, Sam. Get back here and tip us off fast.''

Sam grunted. "What if I run smack into Idaho?"

"Don't ask so many questions, dope," Ez snarled at him. "If you run into that rattler, do what you have to. Is that plain enough, or shall I write it down?"

Sam was too eager for the adventure to take instant offense. He looked questioningly at Stevens.

Pat shook his head. "No—whatever you do, don't throw down on Towner," he cautioned flatly. "It is possible you might run into him, if he's laying low." He was thinking hard. "If that happens, let Idaho think he's capturing you, Sam; and then watch him like a hawk. With you as a witness, he'll either try to get those kids apart and murder them, or he'll stall. That'll give us a little time."

Ez was watching the expression on Sam's face with a malicious grin. "Don't like the sound of it, hey?" He chuckled. "Maybe you better let me go—"

"Go to thunder!" Sloan turned his back on his lanky tormentor. Listening carefully to Pat's final instructions, he hitched his gunbelt up over his tight-fitting overalls and turned away. For all his rotund bulk, Sam could display agility at need; Lackey opened his hooded eyes wide at the way the portly little man stepped behind a nearby rock and seemed to evaporate into thin air.

"What if he don't find a thing, Stevens?" Ez fretted.

"He will," Pat coolly predicted. "I've been watching our friend Bart. He's as jumpy as a cat. If he didn't know what to expect, he wouldn't give a whoop."

Ez favored the renegade with his malign scrutiny. "That's right. We know what to expect from him. While I'm about it, I'll just make sure he don't give us no grief."

Lifting his riata down off the saddle horn, he ordered Lackey to dismount. When the other reluctantly did so, Ez trussed him up securely and tumbled him between two rocks. "Ought to shove an old sock in your face," the lanky tracker grumbled. "But I won't. Just let fly with a yell or two, and see what you get for it."

Pat meanwhile was keeping watch on Sam's progress.

He caught one brief glimpse of the little man some distance down the slope, but that was all. Sam was, in fact, being extra cautious. This was a game at which he was adept. Slithering from rock to rock, he scanned his surroundings sharply before each move, and the lengthening shadows of sunset did not panic him in the slightest.

He circled the first outlying shed warily and, sticking to the brush, wormed steadily on. He was making for the rear of the main collection of buildings now. Again and again he froze to peer cautiously out.

A glimpse between two sagging structures showed him the short main street. It was empty. Such broken steps and window sills as he could see from here were coated with dust. A ghostly hush lay over the vacant buildings. He had just stolen forward, reaching the rear of a sun-blasted store, when a hollow crash near at hand all but made him jump out of his skin.

Tense and ready to scuttle for cover, Sam got a grip on himself. A faint eerie creak provided the answer to what it was that startled him. Minutes ago he had noted the rise of an evening breeze rustling the brush—half of the warped, sagging doors in You Bet were probably aswing.

Now that he had reached town, he was puzzled where to begin. The idea of examining these crazy buildings methodically, one by one, gave him the chills. "Wish I had let Ez tackle this job, he's so smart," he grumbled to himself.

For all his growing uneasiness, it was not like him to give up in a difficult situation. Taking fresh stock of his surroundings, he peered through the windows and back door of the store, making sure it was abandoned, and stole on to the next rattletrap building.

Here a doorless cellar hole gaped under the crumbling foundation. Sam's fleshy jowls quivered. Anything from rattlers to a bear might have taken up its abode in such a cave, and he had no taste for inquiring into the matter. A tossed pebble disappearing into the blackness seemed to settle the point.

The upper floors posed yet another enigma. Sam satisfied himself there were no recent boot tracks in the dust of the ground floor and, passing the place up, took time for another close surveillance of the open street.

This time he could see it better. He made out a tumble-down wreck of a building which once must have been the chief saloon of You Bet. Across its crazily tilted porch ran a faded sign with letters missing: G LD NUG ET. Beyond it stood a solid brick structure with a stone facade, startlingly sound in the midst of all this havoc. A glance told Sam that it must be the bank building.

He studied it attentively, for it offered the most likely hideout for anyone holed up in the deserted town. But the sheet-iron fire door sagged ajar, the barred windows were completely broken out, and the place showed no more signs of occupancy than any other.

He would have to scan it at length in detail, but now he withdrew to the rear of the buildings on that side of town. Standing for long minutes at a back corner, he listened in vain for any other sound than the faintly wailing wind. Dense as this strange silence was, he could not get over the feeling of a hidden presence perhaps watching his every move.

The last flicker of sunlight faded off a roof gable, and the light in the town darkened by one full shade. It reminded Sloan that time was fleeting. For a second he considered showing himself and waving his friends forward without ado. Then his head went up, his jaw taking a curious tilt of determination.

He crept across a sage-tufted open space to the next building in the row. In strange contrast to the rest of these places, he found it boarded up at the rear, the door tight shut. This stopped him dead in his tracks for a full five minutes. Then, wary of making any noise whatever, he pressed on toward the far corner seeking an open window. He was within six feet of the door when suddenly it flew open from inside, and a man stepped out.

Elderly, with a lined and seamed face and hawk eyes, he took Sam's measure in a flash, leveling a gun at his midriff before the little man found time to break out of his frozen surprise. "Hold it right where you are," came the grating command, in undoubted accents of authority. "Just don't make a move if you value your hide, buster!"

18.

SAM's first fleeting thought was that he had allowed himself to be taken by one of Idaho Towner's confederates far more quickly than he had expected or intended. Looking closer as he stood motionless, he realized that he had never seen this man before. But he did not make the mistake of starting to lower his arms.

"Okay, oldtimer. You got me," he allowed gruffly. "Mind telling me what this is all about?"

The shrewd eyes probed him unmercifully. "The charge is loitering on private property," came the uncompromising response. "You Bet is getting altogether too crowded to suit me. Now I aim to break it up!"

Sam was baffled. He could not connect the appearance of this cleancut old rawhide with Idaho's crowd. The man's words had reminded him of nothing so much as a salty law enforcement officer.

"Hold it a second," he brought out quickly. "If you take me for a prowler, neighbor, there could be a reason. Mind telling me who you are?"

"Name's Tooker." There was no softening of the leathery face. "I've been marshal of this town for a good many years. If you didn't know that, you know it now."

It crossed Sam's mind that the old fellow must be unhinged. If he was actually living in You Bet, it was highly probable that he was alone. But Sam knew he had to play along with him or suffer a fatal delay in his own plans.

"That accounts for it then," he began smoothly. "I'm Sam Sloan, Tooker—from over in Powder Valley. Never had occasion to visit your town before. My loss, I can see that."

Tooker didn't bother to acknowledge the informal introduction. "Go on."

"You must know Marshal Ed Roman," pursued Sam quickly. "He's out here in the San Juan country now after an owlhoot named Idaho Towner—"

"Heard of 'em both." Tooker's nod was curt. "So what?"

"Maybe you've heard of Ducks Durgen too. He runs a store over in the San Rafaels." Sam had grown quietly confidential. "Towner kidnapped his girl, Tooker, and he's holding her here in You Bet." He waited for this to have its effect.

The self-styled marshal grunted. "Could be. I don't pretend to know all that goes on here in town. . . . Just how do you hook up with this, Sloan?" he asked keenly.

Sam explained that he and his partner Ezra were working with their friend Pat Stevens, sworn in as a deputy U.S. marshal by Roman for the purpose of apprehending Towner. "Bobby Durgen was a witness to Lyte Majors' killing, if you've heard of that yet. Idaho figures to finish her and young Kit Majors to shut their mouths. Stevens is trying to grab him first and save their lives."

Tooker's eyes were hard. "I'm still waiting—"

"Ain't you got it yet?" Sam jerked out with a rush. "We traced Idaho and those kids here to You Bet, and we got to close in on him before Towner can finish his dirty work." He allowed himself a shade of impatience. "I'm trying to spot that wolf's hideout, Tooker. And you're holding me up!"

Although he entertained certain delusions, hermit-like existence had not made a fool of Ab Tooker. He went outside occasionally for supplies, and he was not deaf to such news of outlaw activity as he could pick up.

"I have talked to Lyte Majors a time or two, and I know his boy," he vouchsafed. "Same goes for Durgen. What makes you think Idaho Towner came to a place like You Bet where him and them youngsters would be recognized right off?''

Sam saw that the old fellow clung tenaciously to the fiction that this sadly deserted place was still a going concern. He had to talk fast to make an impression. ''Probably Idaho figures that folks will be too busy here to notice him much,'' he humored him. ''He's right about you, Tooker—unless you make up your mind in a hurry!''

Old Ab had lowered his gun at last. ''Reckon I'm obliged to look into this, if it does interfere with other duties,'' he allowed. ''Just remember you're on probation till I learn more about it.''

Sam masked a smile. ''We better get moving while it's still light enough,'' he urged mildly. ''If Idaho catches on that anybody's interested in him, he might pull out during the night.''

Tooker delayed, obviously making up his mind. Finally he nodded. ''We can take a look around.''

''Hold it, Tooker.'' Sam caught his arm as he started to turn away. ''Towner knows me. He'll go for his hardware at the first glance, and it won't matter to him if you're in the way. So watch your step.''

''Like that, eh?'' Having been a law officer of no mean stature in his day, old Ab was unimpressed. ''No matter. Just stay behind me, and we'll play it cagey.''

Sam realized that Tooker would know the logical places in this deserted rat's nest to look for a hiding outlaw. ''You're the doctor. Just remember we got to separate Idaho from those kids in a hurry,'' he warned.

Tooker's voice was dry. ''I'll try to remember.'' Turning abruptly, he led the way through an alley into the rear of a sagging shed whose big main door leaned ajar. Here he paused, with Sam at his elbow, and together they peered out into the empty street. Boards torn off the ramshackle buildings lay in the dust, and manifestly no vehicle had moved out there for months, if not years. Even the plank sidewalks were rotting away. The self-appointed town marshal, however, appeared to note nothing unusual.

"Idaho ain't around just now," he grunted. "Could be he's put up over in the hotel and sticking close to the bar—" He broke off. "How many of his gang are with him?"

It was a question which had been bothering Sam for some time. Surely the wily renegade would post a watch—even in this empty town—if any was available.

"Ain't sure. Idaho did have a couple of hombres with him." Tersely Sam outlined the abortive brush with Towner at Gabe Marsh's horse camp. "Ed Roman grabbed one of Idaho's pals, and Stevens is holding another. If there's more, we'll run into them fast enough."

Tooker soberly considered. Fumbling briefly in a shirt pocket, he took out something which he fastened on his sagging vest. Sam saw that it was a tarnished law badge. "Want 'em to know what they're up against," Ab muttered.

Waiting impatiently, Sam peered out through the shed doors toward the bank. It was closer now, standing across the street thirty yards away. It was a two-story place, its empty windows gaping like the eye sockets of a skull. Next door to it, on the side opposite the sagging Gold Nugget Saloon, rose an even more imposing building.

Three stories high, with an open porch running across the front all the way up, its support posts were decorated with crumbling scrollwork and a length of sagging lattice here and there. This was obviously the one-time hotel. YOU BET HOUSE, read the faded lettering on a hanging sign, both of the letter O's raggedly torn out by gunfire.

At first glance, the building appeared absolutely vacant. Plank ends jutted haphazardly from the gaping windows; part of the high roof hung crazily over one side; and a broken chair lay before the open front door. The dark interior looked more like a mysterious cavern the more Sloan studied it. Suddenly he got the strong feeling that something lay in wait over there.

"How'll we reach that place without showing ourselves?" he asked.

"Come on." Tooker motioned him back. Moving out of the shed the way they had come, it was plain the old fellow knew what he was about. Methodically he worked along the rear of these tumbledown buildings, approaching each vacant doorway as if expecting someone to step out. Remembering his own unheralded meeting with Tooker, Sam did not find this exaggerated caution unnecessary.

Ab was agile and remarkably quick. Leading the way, he slipped down alleys cluttered with fallen boards and beams, and once he stepped through an open window to pass on through a dusky store interior in which empty cans and bottles were strewn about. When next they moved into the open, Sam saw that they had reached the upper end of town.

Creeping down along a wobbly board fence, Tooker had another look at the silent street. "We'll cross here," Ab announced. "Walk natural, so nobody will notice."

As they crossed to the far side of the street, Sam found the eerie desolation hard to face. He stole a look downstreet toward the bank without detecting any sign of life. This, however, was no proof that they had not been spotted by some watcher at door or window. As they passed once more into the cover of the sagging structures, he could not help wondering if they were walking straight into an ambush.

"What makes you think Idaho's in that hotel?" he muttered uneasily.

Tooker shrugged. "Where else would you go in a strange town?"

Weary of humoring the strange quirk in Tookers mind that You Bet was still inhabited, Sam had to restrain himself from lashing out at the old man in sour sarcasm. Tooker was, after all, totally unexpected support, and the success of this venture might yet depend on his intimate knowledge of the weird place.

"Towner's too smart to take prisoners to a hotel," Sam argued. "He'll look for a lonely corner where he can box 'em up."

Tooker weighed this deliberately. "That's a good point," he allowed. "Could be we'll be able to figure out just where that is."

With the growing conviction that this oldtimer was hopelessly crazy, Sam followed his footsteps, finding it hard to keep from treading on the other's heels. Nearing the hotel, Tooker halted at the back corner of a shed to scrutinize the rear wall of the place. Here, as in front, the hotel presented an unbroken aspect of desolation. But the old rawhide was not satisfied, and wormed forward for a better look. His attention appeared to be fastened on the upper floors—Sam was unable to guess why. A rattletrap stairway had once run up the back, but the wooden steps were broken out of each flight, in some places for a dozen feet or more.

Studying this depressing sight, Tooker shook his head. "Go on back—" Turning around, he directed Sam along the broken board fence of a one-time corral, which forced them for some distance up the rough slope. At last the fence halted for sheer inability to progress farther through the ragged rocks of the canyon slope. Ab waved his companion onward through the gaps, and now the stocky man saw that they were taking a wide detour across the back of the hotel.

"On your knees now," grunted Ab.

Sam obeyed without protest. But, pausing to gaze through a crevice as he crawled along behind the rocks, he all but vented a snort of exasperation. This far up the slant, they were nearly on a level with the second floor of the rickety hotel building. With windows smashed out and doors blown wide, Sam found that he could see all the way through a long blank hallway from back to front, with the gable of a rotting roof visible on the far side of the street.

It was apparent that for years the hotel had not been occupied by anything but rats and birds. Suddenly, all this useless creeping about seemed utter folly to Sam, and worse—a criminal waste of time. He was about to get to his feet and express his disgust when he encountered Tooker's narrow regard. Those pale blue pupils were like knifeblades.

"Get along, you." There was a snap of authority in the old man's whisper. Abruptly changing his mind, Sam crawled on. There was an urgency in his movements now;

he was anxious to play the farce out and have done with it. Ab motioned him into a downward-slanting gulley. Descending cautiously to avoid a noisy clatter of rubble underfoot, they came out near the corner of the bank building.

Tooker halted Sloan peremptorily and again had his look at the enigmatic hotel. Obviously, the empty view did not please him. "Ain't but one door to the bank," he muttered. "We'll slip down along this side, and maybe we can sneak in."

"In the *bank?*" Sam was visibly annoyed. "What for?"

Tooker gave him a frigid stare. "You're still in my custody, if I've got to remind you, mister—"

"Only hope you know what you're doing," Sam snapped, "because it won't stay light too much longer!"

He could not help asking himself what Pat Stevens and Ezra might be doing now. Not once had he caught any glimpse of movement that suggested their advance; yet if they were waiting for him to produce action, under these circumstances he was fearful of the result.

Stealing silently around the piles of debris along the blank brick wall, Sam came to the front corner of the bank with Tooker at his back. Ab prevented him from stepping into the open, and once more they surveyed the street with care. There was no sign of life whatever.

"It's fifteen feet or so to that bank door," Tooker droned softly. "Step out and make straight for it—and don't kick no pebbles!"

Sam did as he was told, his eyes busy. He could hear Tooker following close at his heels. They reached the entrance, with its sheet-iron fire door partly ajar, and nothing whatever happened. For a moment Sam thought there would be a jarring screech of rusty hinges if he was forced to push the door wider to admit his ample girth. Somehow he squeezed through, treading on crumbled mortar. Tooker stepped in behind him.

It was gloomy in here, with little light from the small, high window openings. Water-stained heaps of papers lay about, and a scurry of mice halted them ten feet from the door, frozen and listening.

In the midst of this profound quiet the iron door abruptly clanged shut behind them, and they heard the rasp of a bolt shot from the outside. Sam's scalp crawled.

"That's Towner!" he whipped out. "Hanged if Idaho didn't spot us, after all—and now he's got us penned in." He whirled on Ab accusingly. "You would make us step into this!"

"Seems like it." Tooker was unemotional. "Anyway, we'll look around while we're here."

There was nothing of note on the ground floor, the bank counters and cages having been removed long ago. Anxious as he was to find an exit, Sam knew it was practically hopeless. He saw Tooker pause before a basement doorway.

"I'll just look down into the vaults," Ab said.

Sam was close behind as he started down. It was like a dungeon here; they had to feel their way. There were dividing walls, and Sloan stumbled over more heaps of moldy papers. The air was dank.

Tooker struck a match, and they saw the heavy vault door. It was pushed nearly shut. Though bars and bolts had rusted, it took all of Sam's strength to pull the heavy door back. The match flickered dimly. Ab dropped it, about to turn away, when Sam cried out, "Something there in the corner, Tooker!" He rushed over, stumbling into a prone form.

"Somebody lying here! Strike another light!"

A second match flared, revealing Kit Majors bound and gagged, his worried eyes wide. Dropping to his knees, Sam quickly worked the gag out of his mouth. "Cripes, boy! So this is where Idaho dumped you. Where's Bobby?"

"I don't—know for sure." Kit drew a sobbing breath. "Untie me, Sloan! We've got to work our way out of here and reach Towner fast, before it's too late."

There was no denying this grim necessity, Sam thought as he worked at the knots. But how?

19.

IF SAM was wondering desperately what his partner and Stevens were up to while Idaho Towner was trapping him in the bank, Pat was returning the compliment with interest. After making sure that Lackey was bound and helpless, he and Ez took turns watching You Bet for a good half-hour without detecting any signs of activity whatever.

Ez at length shook his head dubiously. "You told Sam to let Idaho grab him—and Towner won't be sending out no notices. I'm going down there, boy."

Stevens took one brief squint at the declining sun and nodded. "We'll both go."

Ten minutes later they were approaching the rear of the first buildings. As the distance shortened, they scanned every detail of the empty town. "Kind of queer we don't see hide nor hair of Sam down there," growled Ez uneasily.

They reached a point from which they could see all the way down the length of the deserted main street. Its blank silence was puzzling, and Ezra rose from behind his rock for a clearer look. For two minutes he stood in full view of half the windows of You Bet, but still there was no response. This made the lanky tracker bold.

"We could be wasting time we'll never get back," he rasped. "I'm for pushing right on in there—"

Stevens took only seconds to reach a decision. "It will soon be dark if we work the same way Sam did," he returned flatly. "Let's go."

Rising, they made directly for the end of the street.

Only the dead silence caused them to avoid the broken boards and empty cans lying about; and habitual caution made them move forward fifty feet apart.

Stevens was taking careful note of the empty business buildings, studyng each in turn, when the dead silence was broken by the abrupt crash of a six-gun. A slug slapped a splintered wooden sign directly behind Ezra's head.

"Watch it, Ez! That came from the hotel yonder," Pat sang out, ducking behind a partially collapsed water barrel.

"Somebody awake in this town after all." Coolly Ez strode across to take refuge at the corner of a sagging store porch. "See him, Stevens—?"

Pat had not. Taking deliberate aim, he sent a shot into the shadows of the hotel gallery, and they heard a tin sign resound hollowly. "Thought I saw a movement. We'll work up that way—but watch it close, Ez!"

Edging forward, they pressed on toward the crazily leaning three-story structure. Getting a clearer view across its facade, Stevens sent a slug whistling in through a gaping lower window. He caught the flash of a spitting reply.

"He's in the old bar on the corner," he called across to Ez. "Probably he figures we'll never smoke him out of there."

Although it meant braving a chance shot at any moment, the pair immediately closed in. Whoever had shot at them was bitterly determined to hold them at bay and now kept up a steady firing. Crouching behind a flimsy wooden railing, Ez cursed as he slapped away a flying splinter that had torn his black flatbrim.

"Ain't but one man over there," he jerked out angrily. "Shall we rush the place?"

Pat promptly ruled against this. With only themselves to consider, it might have been worth a try. But Stevens still hoped to identify their adversary, if possible; or failing that, to obtain some clearer idea of what they were up against. Hugging the side of a broken ore wagon, he took careful aim, firing again through the shadowy window of the hotel saloon; this time he heard the slug rip into the heavy bar inside.

The answer was a triple crash of gunfire, peppered with savage invective. Snatching off his Stetson, Pat raised his head cautiously. "Hello in the bar," he called out clearly. "Where's Bobby Durgen, Idaho? We want her—"

"Hell with you, Stevens! Pull out, or you'll never see her alive," came the rasping response from the corner of the gloomy bar.

"So it is you, Towner," Stevens tossed back. "Just wanted to make sure we weren't wasting our time."

Idaho swore bitterly at the ruse which had caused him to betray his presence. "You're begging for what I'll give you, mister," he raged. "The same dose I gave Majors and that nosy friend of yours!" He punctuated the threat with slugs that clanged on the rusty iron fittings of the ore box.

Both Pat and Ez had found it ominous when Sam did not promptly get into this fight. True, they had heard no shots; but it was not beyond Idaho to work with a knife, particularly if he guessed himself to be surrounded. They scarcely dared ask themselves whether it meant that both Kit and Sam had already met death.

Ezra's mouth drew into a thin hard line, and his single eye was like ice. "I'm going in there, boy," he threw at Stevens tensely. "You can come or stay!"

Pat was ready for him. "Work around and come in from the other side, Ez," he gave back. "We'll clamp down on this joker in a hurry."

Ducking into an alley, Ez climbed through a crazy window and moved on through the dusky interior, working past the hotel from building to building. Quiet as he strove to make his progress, the creak of a rotten board or scrape of an incautious boot gave occasional evidence of his stealthy movements. At the same time, Pat crawled back away from the wagon box and made a circuit of the old supply store, steadily approaching the unguarded side windows of the bar.

Stevens and Ezra were both keeping a wary lookout for

any confederates Towner might have. But now, as the slow minutes passed and no new guns entered the fray, Pat dared hope the big outlaw had been cornered here alone.

Uneasy silence held the street, and in the You Bet House, Idaho was frantically trying to discover what was going forward. He evidently concluded his best chance was a bold ruse of his own. "Bill! Cass! You, Lackey!" he bawled, loud enough to be heard for a considerable distance. "Watch them windows close now!"

Arresting his advance at the first word, Pat grinned without humor. Towner, unaware that even now his friend Lackey was lying bound and helpless outside the edge of town, had once more clumsily given himself away. Now Pat was certain that Idaho must be alone.

Inching up along the hotel wall as far as the rear bar window, Stevens risked a look. The interior was too dusky to make out anything, but he could see out through the vacant front windows. Then, beyond the door into the hotel office, he glimpsed a moving shadow. His finger was pressing on the trigger when he made out the shape of Ezra's head.

Acting on shrewd impulse, Pat called out harshly, "Close right in, Ez! We've got him!" At the same instant he flipped a thundering shot in at the opening. An unexpected smash and clatter of empty bottles coincided with Idaho's yell of surprise. As Ezra burst through the inner door, the stamp of running boots echoed from a rear room through which the renegade had retreated. Ezra fired, then ducked back to the hotel office through a hallway.

Quickly hoisting himself in at the bar window, Pat dropped to the floor. "Go that way, Ez! Keep him crowded away from the outside doors!" Following Towner's course as nearly as he could judge it, Pat thrust on through one rear room and then a second, without glimpsing the outlaw. Suddenly he caught the scuff of boots from somewhere in the echoing structure. A gun crashed in another room, and Ezra bawled out. Pat quickly tried one door, then another—without success. He found himself in the narrow hall which ran from front to back, with Ezra's tall frame looming up.

"Where did he go?"

"Don't know—"

Evening light had thinned to the point where little vision was possible in the gloom of the hotel. It was plain that in this mysterious catacomb Idaho Towner had agilely eluded them for a moment; Pat was by no means sure, however, that he had made good his escape.

In the breathless pause which fell, they heard an unmistakable creak and groan of boards from directly overhead. Ez ran to the main stairway and peered up. "Stay there," Pat threw at him. "There must be a back stairs here somewhere. We'll corner him on the next floor!"

Idaho heard them coming. This time the outlaw's running steps sent dust and dirt rattling down and made the whole frame of the hotel shudder slightly—and then came a silence, broken by Ezra's boots as he raced upward. It took Pat a minute or two to locate the rear stairway. Probing the dusk overhead, he took a step or two, paused, and then fired a warning shot, the detonation echoing thunderously in that confined space.

A moment later he and Ez met in the upper hall. "Try those side rooms," ordered Pat sharply. He kicked back a door on his side of the hall, and a puff of stale dust blew out. It was too dark to examine tracks on the floor.

Ez reappeared, gun in hand. "No dice," he rasped. "Unless he's crawled into a crack."

Together they tried a large room which turned out to be double-doored. A faint scurry behind a closet door startled them both before an enormous rat sprang out and darted across the floor.

Wheeling back, they were turning toward the front of the building when a door squeaked. A bulky form loomed vaguely in the gray shadows. A gun cracked, and splinters flew from the plank wall between them.

Both fired. But Idaho had thrown himself aside. He burst into a side room, forcing the door shut in their path

as they sprang to grapple with him. Again the renegade's
Colt exploded, the slug plowing through the panels.

"Keep him away from the stairs," Pat rapped, wheeling
back. The turns and angles and ells in these upper halls
made it impossible to see for any distance.

Turning the other way, Ez reached the next doorway in
time to meet Towner's brawny bulk charging at him like a
battering-ram. They came slamming together before either
could make a move to prevent it. Caught unawares, Ez
crashed down with Idaho on top. As the racket shook the
building, Stevens flung back in time to snap a slug at the
outlaw just as he was falling.

The ball flew high, tearing Idaho's hat from his head
without touching him. In a twinkling, avoiding Ezra's
desperate grab, Towner rolled aside and scrambled through
the door opposite. The thud of his boots raced on through
toward the front.

Hauling Ez to his feet without ceremony, Pat thrust him
forward. "Down the hall!" he barked. "He's making for
those third-floor stairs!"

The darkness slowed them up. They banged into first
one wall angle, then a second. Fifty feet farther on an
unfinished door opened out. About to burst through this,
Ez abruptly halted, barring the way. "Watch it."

They heard boots thumping upward on rickety stairs. As
Pat moved closer, a loose board came clattering down, and
Idaho fired downward over his shoulder.

"Stay right here—" Pat turned and ran for the rear of
the building. He was back in two or three minutes. "Just
as I thought. No back steps up to the third floor—this is
the only way. We've got him trapped now!"

Ez thrust his hat past the door frame, and a slug nearly
tore it from his hand, despite the gloom. His nod was
grim. "No use trying those stairs now. He figures to stand
us off right here, and it'll pretty near work!"

Pat wasted no time in doubt. "Throw a few shots up
there and keep him busy," he directed.

Ez fired up several times without aim, then wheeled as

he thumbed fresh shells into the cylinder. "Hold on—what'll you do, Stevens?"

Pat sent a slug through the third floor, aiming toward the head of the narrow stairs. He said in a low voice, "I noticed some of these second-floor closets were never finished off. I'll wriggle up through on the beams and take Idaho from behind—"

"Well, maybe." Ezra looked grave. "Just watch what you're about, boy."

Pat fully intended to. Seldom was he as deadly calm as now. "Towner won't stop me. I owe him a slug for Sam. Just let him keep his mind on you for five minutes."

Ez fired upward again and again. "We're coming after you, Towner—" he tried to draw the renegade into altercation.

"Come ahead," sang out the other man defiantly backing his invitation with a rattling fusilade. Another loose plank came crashing and banging down the stairwell, booming hollowly against the walls.

In the bank building next door Sam and Ab Tooker had heard the gunfire, the growing uproar, muffled by the intervening walls. "What can be going on out there?" Sam wondered aloud.

The self-styled town marshal was cool. "Sounds like those friends you spoke about have jumped Towner on their own," he hazarded.

Kit Majors evinced swift alarm. "Idaho must have Bobby with him, Sloan!" he burst out. "She's liable to get hurt if they go on throwing slugs around like this!"

"Cripes! Ain't there no way out of this trap, Tooker?" Sam demanded. "I got to get into that myself!"

Ab turned toward the stairs. "There's a second floor where they have offices," he grunted. "We'll see."

They ran upward, the puncher lurching awkwardly as his circulation slowly returned to normal. There was a stairway in a back hall. The red glow of sunset showed them the way, shining through the high barred windows.

The second floor was a shambles of smashed furniture and debris. Tooker looked the high ceiling over sharply, pointing out the inset well of a trap door that led out to the flat roof. "We can see around if we can climb up there," he suggested.

The tumultuous pound of gunfire lent urgency to their movements. "Grab the table here!" cried Sam. Majors helped to drag it over under the trap door; he scrambled up. "See if you can find a box—"

Ab brought one. "Watch out for the busted board." Without response Kit climbed up on it, thrust back the trap door, and swung up by his elbows.

Sam motioned to Tooker. "You next. I'll give you a leg up."

In a moment or two the three were out on the bank roof. Across the intervening roof of a two-story ell they saw the gaping third-floor windows of the hotel. It was from there that the muffled roar of the gun battle swelled across to them.

"That's from somewhere right inside!" exclaimed Sam tautly. "Pat and Ez must have Towner cornered up there."

"Give me a leg over—" Kit started to scramble down to the intervening roof. "I got to get across!"

"*Hold it, boy!*" Sam took a grip on his arm. "You're not even armed."

"What's the difference?" Majors was in a frenzy now. "If Bobby's there, I got to reach her right away!"

He broke off with a gasp as Bobby Durgen appeared suddenly in one of the hotel windows. Her face white and strained, she tried desperately to wave them back, and they saw that her hands were bound.

"Bobby!" cried Kit piercingly.

She shrank unheeding. Wheeling toward the window, as he rapidly fired backward, came Idaho Towner. As he turned his bloodsmeared face toward the three men on the roof, his wicked gaze fastened on Majors, and he threw up his smoking gun.

Uttering a cry of determination, Bobby wildly sought to knock up the leveled gunbarrel with her bound hands. Idaho slashed at her viciously, and swept sidewise, she sank from sight.

20.

"I'LL have your liver for that, Towner!" bawled Kit, in a rage because he was too far away to protect the girl.

At Kit's cry, Idaho Towner again swept his gun around toward the men on the bank roof. This time there seemed nothing to deflect his dire purpose. As the three threw themselves aside, slugs fluttered between them, narrowly missing. Ab Tooker tried to whip his gun out for a reply, but age had slowed him down.

Sam stretched himself at full length on the roof to present the least prominent target possible, then deliberately drew his gun with the cold intention of drilling the outlaw squarely. But before he could take aim, weapons crashed afresh somewhere back in the hotel. Towner whirled to meet the fresh attack. The movement carried him away from the frameless window, and Sam hesitated, his sight uncertain in the sunset glow.

"Let him have it, Sloan," Majors urged fiercely. "You saw what he did to Bobby! Blow the rat to rags!"

He could not understand why Sam gave him a look of impatient disgust instead of emptying his gun at the outlaw. Three minutes ago Kit had been tragically convinced that the girl was already dead; but now he was in a frenzy lest Bobby sustain as much as a further scratch.

Again the guns hammered in the hotel, and Idaho abruptly disappeared from view as he sprang once more toward the head of the third-floor stairwell. Still seeking to pin the renegade's attention, Ezra had reached in from the floor below, grasping one of the boards which Idaho had thrown down and rattling it vigorously to create the impression of someone clambering upward.

Falling for the ruse, Idaho dashed back to the top of the rickety stairs and unleashed a thundering string of shots. It was too dark now in the enclosed stairway to distinguish any mounting figure, but Idaho was savagely resolved to block this single avenue of approach. He leaned out boldly to kick with all his might at the top stairs. A splintered tread jumped from its supports and clattered through to the lower floor—then another. But it still was slow, awkward work. When Ezra threw a random shot from below, the outlaw flinched back from the buzzing splinters.

By no means done yet, Towner bent to grab up a loose ten-foot plank off the unfinished floor. Running the end of it down the steps at an angle, he got a purchase below the slanting stringer which supported one side of the stairway. Throwing his brawny weight on the upper end of the plank, he had the satisfaction of hearing splintering and the protesting screech of rusted nails drawing.

The upper floors of the structure shuddered and groaned as he bore down. Something tore loose with a splitting crack. The stairway fell in with a hollow crash, planks and loose boards sliding and banging all the way through to the ground floor.

Ez was fearful the ruthless outlaw might yet do something that would cause the whole rickety structure to collapse; but he did not panic as the debris rained down. The now empty stairwell, with part of the side wall torn away, gave him a shadowy glimpse of the upper floor. He drove several shots upward, and heard the stamp of boots as Towner hastily dodged back out of range.

If Idaho thought he had effectively cut off attack from below, however, he was badly mistaken. Quietly busy meanwhile in a back corner of the second floor, Stevens had located an unfinished closet. Propping his feet on the cross-braces and slanting supports, he was slowly but steadily working upward.

Within reach of the ceiling, he felt carefully about the

flat planking, finding out by the application of steady pressure that they were laid loose. Once those third floor planks were lifted or pushed out of the way, he could crawl through. Careful to keep Idaho from hearing the planks being moved, Pat, with some ingenious maneuvering, lifted the first one and slid it back out of the way. The second he simply tipped up on edge and flipped over under cover of the crash and racket from the falling stairway.

Heaving himself up, he elbowed his way through the gap. It was dusky in this corner. The third floor was a mare's nest of angling roof supports. There had been only a rough attempt to divide it into rooms: a partial wall of boards here, and there an unfinished doorway. Peering sharply, Pat caught a suggestion of movement across the gloomy cavern under the roof which a little farther along had torn away and hung outward.

Drawing his gun, he sent a shot across. The unwarning attack from yet another direction drew a yell of fury from the astonished outlaw. Towner wheeled, firing blindly. The bullets punched boards and rattled about, but in this deepening gloom Idaho could make out nothing.

"Throw down your gun, Idaho, or this is your finish!" Pat called harshly.

Towner crouched unseen, and there could be heard the rapid clicking of his gun as he jammed in fresh cartridges. Pat fired again, seeking to rattle him. Meanwhile, Ezra could be plainly heard clambering up through the beams on his own account, determined to be in at the end. Puffing and snorting, he got an elbow over the plank edge and drew his head up. He must have seen some sign of movement, for his gun came up and he fired.

To Towner, it seemed suddenly as if angry foes were closing in on him from every quarter. He sprang up from cover and ran over the rattling plank floor to the front of the place. Pat moved swiftly also, changing position barely in time to see Idaho burst out the door onto the rickety third-floor gallery.

Ez scrambled out on the planks, firing sidewise. The slug barely missed Idaho, striking the outer porch rail and carrying a portion of it away. Towner felt the whole fabric of this sagging gallery tremble ominously under his heavy tread. His desperate glance saw no hope of escape that way; even the gallery support posts would be too infirm to carry his weight, if he tried to slide downward. Springing back close to the wall, he knelt under a frameless window and peered inside.

He did not see Pat and Ez standing in there in the treacherous shadows, but they could clearly make out the outlaw's hatless head silhouetted blackly against the pink evening sky. Pat's bullet grazed the opening, and Ez sent a slug fluttering within inches of Idaho's face.

"Call if off, you fool!" the lanky tracker called out harshly. "We'll blow you plumb off that gallery—"

Towner raked the interior with lead and sank below the opening, turning to crawl along the wall. He could hear the men inside calling sharply to each other.

"Close in fast, Ez," Stevens cried. "There's a door at the other end of the gallery. If he gets back inside, it'll be devil take the hindmost!"

The three on the bank roof meanwhile were keenly aware of the blind duel going forward in the dusk-cloaked hotel. They set about clambering across with the least possible delay. Kit leaped down to the intervening ell, while Sam turned to aid old Ab across. As a consequence, young Majors was the first to make the precarious dash across the slant roof and reach the hotel wall.

Working up the roof slant on hands and knees, Kit grabbed at the third-floor window ledge. Afire with concern for Bobby, who had not appeared again following the blow from Towner, he hauled himself up.

At first he could see only the tumbled heap of the girl's dress on the plank floor. Making a spring, he levered himself through the opening. Wholly indifferent to the slugs tearing and glancing about the interior, if he was aware of them at all, Kit dropped to his knees beside the girl with a cry.

To his amazement and relief, her arms promptly clutched

at him, drawing him toward the planks. "Get down, Kit!" she gasped. "You'll be killed—!"

Flooding exaltation made a lion of him. "Bobby! You're all right? I thought you were—"

Crouching out on the gallery, fear knifing through him as the running steps of Ezra and Stevens made the planks bounce and the whole building shake and tremble, Towner risked a fleeting look in through an adjoining window. It afforded him a clear view as Majors dropped into the room where he had left that troublesome girl after he had knocked her down.

From the time he had made both of them captive, Idaho had been acutely aware of the puncher's dread concern for the girl. Playing cruelly on that fear, with sadistic enjoyment, the renegade had kept them alive far beyond the dictates of sober judgement. Had he shot them down and left them lying on the trail, blazing calculation now told him, he might never have been hounded into this fatal ambush.

Slugs punctured the rotten boards close to his position. Idaho felt a tug at his shirt collar; looking down, he saw it hanging raggedly torn. Desperate now, he stumbled up, firing wildly at his assailants. Brushing the dirt from his eyes after a near miss had all but blinded him, he fired again and again in a wild rage. Creeping steadily closer, barely able to throw himself out of the line of that lethal barrage, Ezra vented a defiant roar and threw down on Idaho at point-blank range.

"Don't smoke him down! We want Towner alive!" Pat yelled at him from twenty feet away.

The bare sense of the words flickered in Idaho's brain. Not for an instant did he believe they spelled reprieve. Yet he was quick to grasp the momentary advantage. Savagely certain that Majors had somehow brought retribution down on him, Idaho blamed Kit and no one else for all his troubles.

Whirling back, he charged at the far door and blundered back inside like a maddened bull. He could see the puncher apparently trying to pick the girl up from the floor. It was nearly pitch dark in here, with only a partial light filtering in from the spaced window openings. Idaho slammed blindly into upright roof supports without being conscious of them; with a trembling clatter, he carried away the two-by-fours, the obstructions not even slowing his charge, so impelling was his fury.

Kit heard him coming. Throwing a look over his shoulder, he read the danger in a flash. Without a gun, he had only his naked fists with which to face an assault. There was barely time in which to tear free of Bobby's clasp, whirl in a crouch, and meet Towner's rush.

"You meddling squirt! I'll finish *you*—" screamed Idaho. Bounding close, he threw up his gun. Majors struck at him, striving without success to deflect his deadly aim.

The dead click of Idaho's hammer on an empty shell came as such a stunning surprise that for an instant neither man was prepared for it. With a roar of hatred and frustration, Towner recovered first, raising the weapon over his head to chop fiercely at his foe.

Kit barely avoided that first blow. He dared not close with the huge outlaw, aware that Idaho could crush him with a single arm. Boldly erect, he sent a rocky fist smashing into Towner's hard face. It held Idaho off for three seconds—and it was all that saved him.

Suddenly Stevens and Ezra came hurtling forward. Pat whirled the renegade back with grunting force. Tearing his gun from his waving fist, Ez tripped him, and Idaho went down with a crash that made the rickety hotel sway alarmingly.

He was not done yet, writhing in his determination to struggle up. Ez and Pat grabbed him and pinned head and shoulders to the trembling floor. Slipping through the window at that moment, Sloan darted forward to sit down heavily on the outlaw's thrashing legs.

A moment more of fruitless struggle, and it penetrated Towner's fogged brain that he was licked. Kit had knelt to help Bobby Durgen sit up. She looked from one to another of these businesslike men with blank disbelief.

"Is—is he—?" She could not manage more at the moment.

It was Ab Tooker, laboriously letting himself through the window, who answered. "I expect he's out of circulation, ma'am," he reassured her dryly. "Been some years now since it's paid off to tear loose around You Bet."

"Think so, eh? You ain't none of you out of this yet," raged Idaho with the implacable venom of a wounded grizzly.

Pat coldly slapped his head down. "Shut up, you . . . Yank his belt and tie his claws down," he directed tersely. Nor did he relieve the pressure of his knees from Towner's flattened shoulder blades while the renegade's arms were being yanked behind his back and firmly secured.

With the hot blood of combat cooling down, Ezra rose to peer uneasily about. "How'll we get out of here without a tumble?" He stamped the quivering floorboards experimentally.

"Hey! Quit that," Sam snapped at him. "You figuring to bring this old trap down on our heads?"

Pat's laugh was jarring. "Idaho kicked the stairs down. It's safest for Bobby to go back across the roofs—and if Towner breaks a rib or two, it won't matter."

Sam nodded, letting the outlaw sit up. "Just enough light left to make it," he opined. "Shall we start?"

Majors was already helping the girl to clamber through the window opening. "Kit, if you hadn't come in time!" she breathed prayerfully, letting herself down into his arms with complete trust. His clutch tightened briefly; then he led her across to the bank roof with great care, boosting her up.

"Wait there," he commanded, turning. "Hey, Stevens— I'll slide down. Then I can drop off and unbolt the bank door. It's fastened now."

Sam and Tooker worked their way across next to await Towner's arrival, while Kit slid cautiously to the roof's lower edge and dropped into the street. A moment later the iron fire door could be heard creaking open.

"All right, Idaho." Stevens thumbed toward the window. "Your turn—and just remember the price on your head is the same, dead or alive."

Idaho had no stomach for a falling death; he let himself over the edge with exaggerated caution. Following, Ez kept a steadying grip on him. Pat watched them inch across, and came after. Idaho was hauled roughly up to the bank roof in swiftly fading light.

Ab Tooker stepped to the trap. "I'll go down first. Stay put till I fetch a light." He lowered himself from sight, and a few minutes later a lantern flickered in the dusky bank. Sam and Kit helped the girl through the trap. Next went Towner, with Pat and Ez bringing up the rear. Ab held up the lantern, with a sagacious look.

"What'll you do with Idaho?" he asked.

While Pat hesitated, Sam hastily introduced the self-appointed marshal of You Bet, commenting approvingly on Ab's unstinting aid. "Is there a stout bolt on that vault in the cellar, Tooker?" he pursued. Tooker said there was. "Fine. Why don't we heave this big bad wolf in there till Ed Roman picks him up, Stevens?" the stocky man inquired.

"Not only that," Pat assented, "but we'll toss Lackey in there with him. One or the other should supply Roman with all the evidence he needs on that Rocky Ford stickup."

Idaho was accordingly hustled below and thrust into the vault. Cracks in the thick walls would afford him plenty of air. Bolting the heavy door, Tooker turned to the others. "Can't invite everybody in You Bet," he announced meticulously. "But if *you* folks will step across the street to my place, I'll stir up a meal after all that hard work."

It suited the Powder Valley trio; but making for the open street, Sam Sloan urged care lest they interrupt Bobby and Kit, moving arm in arm out under the glinting stars. "She's convinced he saved her life—and come to think of it, I expect that's about right," murmured Sam.

Turning toward them as they emerged, the girl clung to Majors in obvious, unabashed worship. But Kit found time to recall their immediate affairs.

"What now, Stevens?" he inquired.

Pat smiled unseen in the thick dust. "We'll get Bobby

back to the store first, all in one piece. Roman should show up there in a day or two, if he isn't there now.''

"That's right. And the reward for Towner will make up handsomely for the wild horses we never caught," added Sam.

"In fact," struck in Ez coolly, "we can go back to the Uncompahgre with that money, and if Gabe Marsh did just as I told him to, we can buy that good roan herd we came here for in the first place."

"But the time you had to spend—" began Bobby, her eyes reflecting the golden glow from the west.

Pat laughed. "We'll chalk that up to making your affairs and Kit's come out even," he said quietly. "Shall we go over and eat Tooker out of house and home? We've still got to haul Lackey down here and chuck him in the cooler. If we can scrape up horses enough, we'll pull out in the morning for Durgen's store and give him a rundown on what's been happening. I reckon he'll be pleased.''

CLASSIC ADVENTURES FROM THE DAYS OF THE OLD WEST FROM AMERICA'S AUTHENTIC STORYTELLERS

NORMAN A. FOX

DEAD END TRAIL	70298-3/$2.75US/$3.75Can
NIGHT PASSAGE	70295-9/$2.75US/$3.75Can
RECKONING AT RIMBOW	70297-5/$2.75US/$3.75Can
TALL MAN RIDING	70294-0/$2.75US/$3.75Can
STRANGER FROM ARIZONA	70296-7/$2.75US/$3.75Can
THE TREMBLING HILLS	70299-1/$2.75US/$3.75 Can

LAURAN PAINE

SKYE	70186-3/$2.75US/$3.75Can
THE MARSHAL	70187-1/$2.50US/$3.50Can
THE HOMESTEADERS	70185-5/$2.75US/$3.75Can

T.V. OLSEN

BREAK THE YOUNG LAND	75290-5/$2.75US/$3.75Can
KENO	75292-1/$2.75US/$3.95Can
THE MAN FROM NOWHERE	75293-X/$2.75US/$3.75Can

Buy these books at your local bookstore or use this coupon for ordering:

Avon Books, Dept BP, Box 767, Rte 2, Dresden, TN 38225
Please send me the book(s) I have checked above. I am enclosing $_____
(please add $1.00 to cover postage and handling for each book ordered to a maximum of three dollars). *Send check or money order—no cash or C.O.D.'s please.* Prices and numbers are subject to change without notice. Please allow six to eight weeks for delivery.

Name _____

Address _____

City _____ State/Zip _____

WES/TRAD 9/88

Please allow 6-8 weeks for delivery